Trying to Live

Trying to Live

Romello Hollingsworth

Print information available on the last page.

Rev. date: 09/01/2017

To order additional copies of this book, contact:
Xlibris
1-888-795-4274
www.Xlibris.com
Orders@Xlibris.com
546719

Black Woman: Don't knock at my door, little child

I cannot let you in/ You know not what a world this is of cruelty and sin/ Wait in the still eternity until I come to you the world is cruel, cruel, child I cannot let you in!/ Don't knock at my heart, little one I cannot bear the pain of turning deaf-ear to your call time and time again!/ You do not know the monster men inhabiting the earth/ Be still, be still, my precious child I must not give you birth.

Chapter 1

Under the dark skies and stars, beneath the full moon, it was a beautiful summer night in the city of Chicago. On every street corner, dozens of city street lights illuminated the streets, alleys, sidewalks, parked cars, houses, and brick apartment buildings along the way in an eastside Chicago neighborhood. Newer model cars, others old were lined up one after another parked on each side of the streets. Moving in every direction throughout the neighborhoods, cars traveled north/south and east/west.

Black people of all ages hung out in the streets on the street corners; while others sat on their porches listening to music, shooting the shit, laughing with each other enjoying the beautiful summer night. Teenage boys were hugged up with their girlfriends comfortably leaning on cars in their neighborhood that wasn't theirs. In most places that disrespectful act may get you shot, but in Chicago, it's the other way around you may get shot for telling a motherfucker to get the fuck off your car.

Young and old black folks were hanging out listening to all types of music ranging Drake, Tyga, Young Money, Chief Keef, 2pac, Gucci Mane, RKelly and even Kelly Rowland.

Surprisingly, Auntie Katherine found a parking spot. With ease, she paralleled parked in a tight spot between two cars directly in front of her sister and neice Lil Bit's apartment building. Smiling at her niece backing in parallel parking, Auntie Katherine popped her collars.

"I Can do this shit in my sleep neicy. Watch this!", Katherine said laughing a wicked chuckle bragging on her parking skills as she whipped her car smoothly between a tight squeeze of two parked cars.

"You always think you're the best there is at everything you do Bitch!" Lil Bit thought to herself unnoticeably rolling her eyes, folding her arms then cracking a halfhearted smile and a laugh faker than Nikki Minaj's ass.

Eyes droopy, mouth frowned downward, Lil Bit returned to her gaze looking straight ahead. No matter how depressed or sad looking Lil Bit's expression was at the time, she always looked adorable. No depressed look could ever make her look ugly. She possessed natural beauty. Her beauty was as natural as her curly hair pulled back in a ponytail. Lil Bit could pass for Ashley Banks off the Fresh Prince of Bel-air. Lil Bit was short and thick. Her long hair, caramel skin complexion and beyonce curves, made her the envy of all the girls in her neighborhood. Imagine Ashley Banks from the hood and top of her class in street smarts; that was Lil Bit's persona live in the flesh. But for a while Lil Bit hadn't been her usual sassy self. She's been troubled, and quiet. Her heart has been heavier than an elephant. Her spirits had been cloudier than Snoop Dogg's smoke room. Lately, she's been very vulnerable and confused.

Turning off the car and radio, Auntie Katherine glanced at Lil Bit noticing her downcast, deep in thought facial expression.

"Neicy Pooh!", Auntie Katherine said gently shaking her.

"Baby—I already told you. Don't let this get to you"

With a stern yet sympathetic facial expression Katherine softly touched Lil Bit's chin and explained her position.

"When me and your mom first moved to Chicago, we were still young as hell.

The big City was new to us; they teased us and called us country girls;

Girls, was jealous of us because of our long hair, good looks and creo background.

All the niggas was trying to fuck us. So we had to be smarter than the next bitch and average motherfucker out here. We had to learn how to survive in Chicago. We had to learn these streets the tricks, and the manipulation, so we did whatever it took for us to survive."

Still looking sad with her eyes downcast, Lil Bit looked up at Auntie Katherine nodding her head assuring Katherine that she understood what she was talking about, but still couldn't understand why her? Katherine continued.

"It seemed like every day, we had to fight nappy head bitches that was jealous of us.", Katherine said shaking her head frowning her face from the reminder of how life was when she and her family first moved to Chicago from Louisiana.

"But eventually they respected us because we held our own. People in the hood use to say those Louisiana girls ain't nothing to fuck with. You feel me neicy. We can't be soft out here.", Katherine said looking at Lil Bit raising her voice a little.

"We had to beat bitches asses. Me your mama and your grandmamma had to get out of that sweet southern Louisiana country girl mentality and adapt to these mean Chicago streets, so we had to be more scandalous than the next bitch or nigga out here.

That's why we're here today...only the strong survive! Me, Marose and Mama held each other's back, we looked out for each other.

Even when mama was getting her ass beat by daddy, with her black eyes and bloody lips and shit, we was there for mama. We stood behind her, when she cried to us—we cried together. Because of us we survived. Although, me and that woman Yo Grandma would fuss and fight and be mad at each other and wouldn't talk to each other for weeks, at the end of the day I loved that woman to death. That's the real boss bitch." Auntie Katherine chuckled feeling Lil Bit's head with more bullshit.

Eyes watery filled with tears, Lil Bit Looked into Katherine's eyes finding it hard to believe that her loving grandpa Mr. Williams would ever lay a hand on her Granny. And hearing Katherine referring to her granny as a boss was crazy as hell compared to the sweet church going woman she known all her life.

But according to Katherine what she was saying was true. Before Lil bit was born, the William's went through some tough times.

Like a student to a teacher, a child to its mother, a church follower to its pastor, Lil Bit absorbed every word that came out of Katherine's mouth. She believed her Auntie Katherine. She loved her family and would do anything in the world for her family. But something wasn't right.

There was a conflict in Lil bit's heart, an unresolved question in her young mind that she didn't understand. The deeper involved she became in the scheme of things with Auntie Katherine, the more confused she was.

"It's all about sacrifice Lil Bit", Auntie Katherine continued.

"The way my mama and your grandmamma Juanita Louise Williams sacrificed her life for us. It's our turn to repay her...Mama and daddy is getting old, and we gotta take care of them",

"You and Marose don't even know the half of what's been going on? Mom knows that Marose is busy working and taking care of you and Savion and she didn't even bother telling Marose about her health and that she's dieing... And you know how your mama is, she worries herself sick so don't say nothing to her about what I told you"

"Ok", Lil Bit whispered, assuring Katherine's secret was safe with her.

"When the time is right...I will tell Marose myself...Mom tells me everything and the cancer is spreading fast...Dad is losing the house, because of mama's hospital bills—their having money troubles...it's all fucked up Neicy...so I been helping daddy pay the mortgage...it's just all crazy Lil Bit.", Katherine shook her head with grief.

Lil Bit wanted to cry, but she stood strong, the thought of losing her grandma had not only saddened her but frighten her to death.

With her head down, Lil Bit pulled on the passenger's door handle to let herself out. Right before Lil Bit opened the door; Reaching between the cleavage her breasts, Auntie Katherine pulled out a wad of money.

"Here neicy, need some money?" Katherine said peeling off a 50 dollar bill and two 20 dollar bills from the wad of money handing the bills to Lil Bit.

"Thanks Auntie"

"No problem...keep your phone on too...I'mma be calling you"

"Ok"

"I love you"

"I love you too Auntie", Lil Bit replied, before jogging a few yards to the entrance doors of her apartment building.

With one of the two keys on a pink heartshaped key chain, Lil Bit unlocked the door to her two bedroom apartment she shares with her Mom, and little brother Savion. The apartment smelled good like flowers and spice. On the end table located by the sofa was Lil Bit's favorite picture. A platinum finished photo frame portrait of her parent's high school prom picture, dressed in a silky shimmery elegant aqua blue dress made up like a beautiful princess, her mom Marose was 7 1/2 months pregnant with her. Lil Bit's dad was tall dark and handsome, dressed in an all white Tuxedo, sporting an aqua blue bow tie matching Marose's prom dress. With his arms wrapped tightly around Marose, his smile shined brighter than the sun.

The baby faced couple in the picture looked happily in love.

Sadly to say, Lil Bit's dad Jon Jon was murdered, when Lil Bit was only 16 months old. The portrait of their prom picture with her in her mommy's belly was the only thing closest to having a family portrait together.

Their apartment was filled with family photos. Hanging perfectly on the wall was a portrait of Mr. and Mrs. Williams, Marose, Auntie Katherine, Lil Bit, and Savion. In the living room just below the portrait on the wall, lying on a plush couch and lightly snoring, Marose was comfortably tucked under a blanket. The dry botanical materials of cinnamon and spice potpourri sat on an expensive large shiny black marble plate. The plate sat at the center of the dining room table in the dining room.

"Mom", Lil bit repeated several times causing Marose to slightly shift her body for a more comfortable position.

"MOM!", Lil Bit said again with frustration in her voice.

"Huh? What Lil Bit?", Marose answered voice groggy. Eyes still shut.

Disappointed and agitated for no reason, Lil Bit looked at her mom sleeping shaking her head.

"Nothing Mom", Lil Bit walked away heading towards her bedroom.

"Come here Shatanya!", Marose shouted calling Lil Bit by her real name.

Turning around, Lil Bit walked back towards the living room.

"It's nothing mom, I was trying to wake you up, but nevermind", Lil Bit said really needing someone to talk to, but couldn't get her mind right to speak.

"I'm up now! What is it?"

"Nothing Mom, Forget it! Go back to sleep"

Staring at Lil Bit, Marose sat up on her elbow with her hand under her chin.

"Girl you woke me up for nothing it better be something."

"Really it's nothing mom", Lil Bit said softly before walking to her room.

Sensing something was bothering Lil Bit, Marose's motherly instincts went into action. For a few moments she wrestled with the thought of what was troubling her babygirl. With a concered look on her face, Marose stared at Lil Bit until she vanished into her bedroom. Over by the closet, a dozen of rainbow colorful female Jordans, airmaxes, adidas, and pumas lined up neatly against the wall.

The 36 inch flat screen TV mounted on the bedroom wall made it the third flatscreen TV in the apartment. Tossing her keys onto her neatly made up bed next to the big stuffed yellow tweety bird, Lil Bit prepared to shower. Sitting on her bed, Lil Bit took off her shoes. From the closet, she retrieved towels, panties, a pajama set, and her favorite soap: Soapy Suds Grapefruit Aloe and body wash bubbling bath. Stripping naked, Lil Bit threw her worn clothes into the dirty clothes bin, put her robe on and headed towards the bathroom.

Walking barefooted, Lil Bit had always liked the feeling of her feet against the soft pink plush bathroom rug matching the pink belle fabric shower curtains in the bathroom. Their bathroom stayed clean and spotless. It smelled like roses most of time, that's only if Lil Bit's lil brother Savion didn't stink it up real bad. She turned the faucet on, placing hand under the running water. Luke warm, warm, hot/warm, within a few seconds the water temperature was just how she liked it—steaming hot. Once the water began showering down splishing and splashing against the floor of the bathtub, Lil took her robe off then entered the shower. While lathering the face towel with soap, tears slid down Lil Bit's butterscotch face. With the face towel now foaming with soap, Lil Bit violently scrubbed her face. The past few weeks she's been acting very strange and those closest to her noticed her peculiar behavior. And only God knows why she opened her mouth under the pouring shower sticking her tongue out scrubbing the soapy towel on her tongue spitting water and soap out of her mouth. Next, she began scrubbing her private parts as tears poured from her eyes. Shaking and crying uncontrollably, the pain in her heart made her legs give out. She skinned her thigh against the porcelain bathtub, when she fell on her ass causing the water to splash and a loud thump to echo in the bathroom. But she was in so much emotional pain, she hardly felt it.

Leaning back against the front round of the bathtub, she sat in a fetal position with **her** arms wrapped around her legs. Her body shook from bouts of uncontrollable weeping, while the showering water splashed against her body. Lil Bit was unable to catch her breath from crying and weeping so hard. After 20 minutes of crying uncontrollably, Lil Bit finally gathered the strength to stand up, get out the shower and dry off. Feeling shameful with her head down, unable to face herself in the mirror, she put on her pajamas then walked to her room. She grabbed the teddy bear that her dad had given her when she was 1 yr old. Getting into bed, she pulled the quilt over her head and body, cuddling with her teddy bear then cried herself to sleep.

Chapter 2

While Lil Bit slept peacefully in her bed, a mile away from her apartment building, D.J. Lightbulb and his drug dealer Meechie was having a Juke Party at the Boys and Girls Club for the young people in their neighborhood.

The Boys and Girls club had been transformed into a nightclub. Glowing and mesmerizing neon lights were flickering in the darkness. Loud Juke Music echoed throughout the basketball stadium. Breaking all the rules of Boys and Girls club, rowdy teenagers were partying and sneaking around, popping mollies, smoking loud blunts, and drinking. D.J. Lightbulb stood on a mini man made stage 4 feet high and 10 feet wide made of blocks of black wood that safely supported him, the speakers, turntables and the rest of his equipment.

"She wanna fuck with a pimp like me she wanna fuck with a pimp like me ♫♫♫♫ she wanna fuck with a pimp like me ♫♫♫♫ she wanna fuck with a pimp like me.", blasted loud as hell from the speakers.

Teenagers were having fun juking, hollering, acting silly and dancing around. Suddenly, the music stopped when D.J. Lightbulb touched something on the turntables. Then he put his mouth close to the microphone.

"WHAT'S GOOD CHICAGO…EASTSIDE STAND THE FUCK UP." causing a hysteri, the kids went beserk hollering out their blocks, clicks, schools, and hoods.

"WHICH SIDE IS THE BEST SIDE?", D.J. Lightbulb spoke into the microphone. "EASTSIDE!",The crowd of kids cheered.

"LOOK AT THE SOUTHSIDE, WESTSIDE, AND SOUTH SUBURB PEOPLE.", D.J. Lightbulb laughed.

"THEY LOOKING LIKE WE FORGOT ABOUT THEM.",

"DON'T WORRY Y'AWL WE AIN'T FORGOT ABOUT YAWL EITHER. WE GOT LOVE FOR EVERYBODY. ALL OF CHICAGO. IT'S A CHICAGO THANG, SOUTHSIDE MAKE SOME MOTHERFUCKING NOISE!", Lightbulb hollerd voice blarring from the speakers causing the kids to cheer after calling their side of Chicago.

"NOW WESTSIDE MAKE SOME MOTHERFUCKING NOISE.",

"AND LAST BUT NOT LEASE IS HARVEY, EAST HEIGHTS, PARK FOREST AND THE REST OF THE SOUTH SUBURBS IN THIS BITCH MAKE SOME MOTHERFUCKING NOISE.", Although there were some cheers, the Eastside cheers were much louder than the rest because it was a their neighborhood.

"AS YAWL MAY KNOW MY NAME IS D.J. LIGHTBULB AND WE CAME HERE TO HAVE SOME FUN AND PARTY WITHOUT THE ALL THE DRAMA AND BULLSHIT. ARE Y'AWL READAY TO HAVE SOME FUN", Jumping up and down, the teenagers cheered for a drama free night.

"THAT'S WHAT'S UP YAWL? YAWL KNOW WHAT TIME IT IZ...IT'S WARZONE TIME!!" D.J Lightbulb said reversing a record on the turntables.

"What dat do?", the lyrics from the record played before he stopped it again. "ARE Y'ALL READY FOR THE WARZONE?"

"YEAH!!!", teenagers cheered from the crowd.

"OK THIS IS HOW IT'S GONNA GO DOWN... FIRST PRIZE WINNER GET $150 FOR THE BEST JUKE DANCING TONIGHT. TONITE CONTESTANT ARE.", D.J. Lightbulb said into the microphone.

"OUT FROM SOUTHSHORE, RESPRESENTING KING HIGH SCHOOL. I WANT Y'ALL TO GIVE IT UP AND MAKE SOME NOISE FOR BIG MOTHERFUCKING TED." Big Ted stood about 5 feet 8 inches tall weighing 265 pounds, but his big ass could juke his ass off. Before, D.J. Lightbulb announced the last dancer he announced 3 other dancers: 1 male and 2 other females.

"AND LAST BUT NOT LEAST REPRESENTING THE L.O.A CLICK. WE GOT MS. REDBONE. BETTER KNOWN AS LEMON REPRESENTING 75TH STREET. GIVE IT UP FOR FINE ASS LEMON."

Lemon was the 3rd member of the L.O.A Ladies of Action girls dance click. High yellow with big pretty eyes, her booty and curves would make Beyonce jealous.

Lemon looked innocent and sweet, but her attitude was so fucked up, she'll make any diva off bad girls club and love and hip hop Atlanta look like Mother Theresa. At only 17 years old, Lemon was living a life more fas tand glamorous than any woman twice her age. For the past 7 months she had been dating 26 years old drug dealer named Meechie. He gave her any and everything her adolescent heart desired. And in return she gave him unlimited access to her body.

Lemon was dressed in an all black spaghetti strapped top showing off her gold herring bone necklace resting on her cleavage, wearing a red one legged coochie cutter tights, showing off her new Chinese dragon tattoo on her right thigh. Her nail polish game was on point. The red and black Bengal tiger firey designed on her fingernails matched her sexy outfit.

She paced around getting ready for battle, while the other dancers prepared themselves as well. "MAKE SOME NOISE FOR THE INFAMOUS LEMON.", Lightbulb hollered into the microphone then spun the record. "Gon and drop it down."

After 20 minutes of the contestants battling in the warzone, Lemon and Big Ted received the loudest cheers from the crowd and was battling for the winner's spot. Like New York beatstreet break dancers, competition style battling, one after another Lemon and Big Ted went at it. "Bang bang bang…skeet skeet skeet ♫♫♫♫…bang bang bang…skeet skeet skeet…bang bang bang…skeet skeet skeet ♫♫♫♫…bang bang bang…skeet skeet skeet… bang bang bang…skeet skeet skeet…bang bang bang…skeet skeet skeet." Big Ted was getting ready to hit the dance floor for the fourth time tonight determined to win.

When he hit the dance floor, his adidas on his feet began moving so fast to the beat, a Cheetah couldn't catch him.

"GO TED!…GO TED!…GO TED!…GO TED!…GO TED!", The crowd cheered as D.J. Lightbulb mixed the records "BANG BANG BANG… SKEET SKEET SKEET."

With "GON AND DROP IT DOWN…BANG BANG BANG… SKEET SKEET SKEET…BANG BANG BANG SKEET SKEET SKEET… GON AND DROP IT DOWN…BANG BANG BANG SKEET SKEET SKEET…BANG BANG BANG SKEET SKEET SKEET…BANG BANG BANG SKEET SKEET SKEET…GON AND DROP IT DOWN"

The mix repeatedly played, as Big Ted entertained the crowd moving his feet swiftly and perfect to the beat. His big chubby body bounced up and down like a basketball. For a big boy, Big Ted had heat. By the sound of the crowd cheering for Big Ted, D.J. Lightbulb might as well had hand over the cash to Ted's chubby hands. Big Ted didn't break a sweat. After he was done, he confidently strutted within the warzone circle like a champion boxer who had just won a title fight as the crowd cheered and congratulate him girls trying to hug him and his boys giving him high 5's.

With a displaced look on her face, Lemon had to do something. How was she going to top Big Ted's performance.

D.J. Lightbulb spun the next mix on the turntables.

"Let me see you juke it ♫♫♫ Let me see you juke it ♫♫♫ Let me see you juke it",

Lemon sashayed within the warzone circle moving her body from side to side stumping her feet so hard that her booty jiggled, causing the boys in the crowd to look at her like hungry dogs with their tongues out. Then D.J. Lightbulb switched the mix up.

"LET ME BANG ♫♫♫♫...LET ME BANG ♫♫♫♫...LET ME BANG ♫♫♫♫...

LET ME BANG...LET ME BANG." Like an 80's break dancer ready to pop lock and drop it, Lemon pulled both arms in front of her body. "1...2...3 Bang", She whispered to herself before her body went into convulsions like a Christian woman catching the holy ghost in church.

"LET ME BANG ♫♫♫...LET ME BANG ♫♫♫...LET ME BANG ♫♫♫... LET ME BANG...LET ME BANG."

The music blasted loud as hell in the auditorium as Lemon surprisingly did some of her best footworking; Lemon's milkshake definitely brought all the boys to the yard. The infamous leader of the L.O.A girls spun around, kicking her feet up, as she burned the dance floor with her sexy moves causing the teenage boys go beserk and lose control. With their tongues out laughing like laughing hyena's acting like out of control grown men at the strip club hawking and oogling over sexy strippers, the boys had fun.

Jealous girls and Lemon's hater's in the club frowned, when Lemon began doing splits and humping the floor, but the boys lost their minds. At the end of her dance routine Lemon bent over and jiggled her booty. Even Lightbulb had to catch a glance, after she finished "THAT'S WHAT'S UP GIVE IT UP FOR LEMON!", D.J. Lightbulb said.

The crowd of boys cheered for her as Lemon's boyfriend Meechie and his goon Black approached the mini booth, where Lightbulb was standing in front of his turntables and microphone.

"ALRIGHT ALRIGHT! GIVE IT UP FOR ALL THE DANCERS TONITE! LEMON, KESHIA, LARRO, FATTY AND BIG TED, AIN'T NO LOSERS EVERYBODY GOT IT IN TONITE.", Cheering and clapping, the crowd of teenagers shouted out their favorite dancers...

"ALRIGHT ALRIGHT YAWL IN ABOUT 10 MINUTES WE'RE GOING TO ANNOUNCE THE $150 WINNER OF THE WARZONE.", Lightbulb announced as he scrolled through his library of songs on his laptop, finally finding a song.

"I'M ABOUT TO SLOW IT DOWN WITH YA BOY OMARION'S SONG SLOW DANCING MIX I DID FOR Y'ALL I WANT Y'ALL TO BANG THAT SHIT GO BURN THAT SHIT FOR FREE ON ITUNES.

BE RIGHT BACK IN A MINUTE CHICAGO.", D.J. Lightbulb said putting on the mix afterwards signaling for Meechie and Black to come have a seat on the side of the stage steps.

"What's good Big Meechie?", D.J. Lightbulb said giving Meechie some dap. Meechie was medium height. Wearing all black and smelling like Christian Dior cologne with a black stocking cap on his head, a black shirt under a black leather vest, black leather jeans, with two solid gold chains hanging from his neck. He chewed gum. "My nigga D.J. Lightbulb what's good Fam?", Meechie replied with a his own style and swagger.

"I'm trying to get like you fam.", Meechie added.

"What nigga? Stop playin", Lighbulb laughed.

"I'm dead ass nigga, I'm in the wrong line of business, I need to start D j-ing. You're the hottest D.J. in Chicago, stop fronting nigga! You got dem bandz. Let ya boi hold 20 racks you know I'm good for it."

D.J. Lightbulb was flabberghasted. He didn't believe Meechie wanted to be like him. With a puzzle look on his face, he shook his head.

"Stop it right now Meechie, you know you're the man, the only reason you pulled out the burnt orange Charger on 26's was because you didn't feel like driving the Lex or that new four door Ford F150 with like 20 miles on it, stop fronting nigga.", Lightbulb laughed.

"Believe me you don't want to be like me." Meechie couldn't top D.J. Lightbulb's response, he knew he was the man. He knew that his money was longer than the Mississippi River, but people with legit lifestyles, such as D.J. Lightbulb, he admired. In fact, Meechie secretly wished he could have a promising legal career. He hated his lifestyle. The constant looking over his shoulders and the distrust he felt around the people he associated with. Meechie knew that if he made any false move or get caught slipping one time fucking with the wrong person could either put him 6 feet under in the grave yard or land him in jail for the rest of his life.

"Yeah you got me man!", Meechie laughed.

"So what's going on with you Lightbulb. Stop playing me man…I told you that I'm ready to take this shit to the next level bro."

"Yeah Meech man, I know how bad you wanna get in with me.

I been talking to Ciara's and Chris Brown's manager.

We putting together somethings so this Chicago Juke thang can go international. I'm on some next level shit. You know me Meech!"

"But you ain't fucking witcha Boyyy!", Meechie replied.

"I been telling you to come fuck with me man.

I got you fam 30, 40, 50, 100 racks. Whatever nigga?

Lets do this and stop talking about it. I got you fam."

For the most part, D.J. Lightbulb financial support came from family, financial institutions, business investors, and trusted friends. D.J. Lightbulb had grew up with Meechie. He had had nothing against him, but he knew from experience not to get Meechie, any drug dealer or any street hustler for that matter involved in his music thing. Meechie had an infamous reputation on the streets ranging from Chicago all the way up to Minnesota. People who had owed him money came up missing and was never heard from again. Throwing shows, doing mixtapes, and birthday parties for Meechie, drug dealers, or any gang banger was as far as D.J. Lightbulb would go. Anything beyond that, such as borrowing twenty to fifty thousand was asking for trouble. Losing a drug dealer's money was like walking on a field with landmines. Friend or not, one wrong step could cost D.J. Lightbulb his life. Although Meechie's offer was tempting, Lightbulb would always find away to brush him off.

"It ain't that Meech man…I just thought you were too busy doing yo thang kid!…I thought maybe you didn't have time for this little money.

What I make in a month doing this D.J. shit…you make in a day."

"Stop playing Lightbulb…you know you make way more money than that…nigga you trying to be greedy", Meechie frowned his face…I'm the same way nigga!", Meechie laughed.

"Naww! Forreal tho fam…no bullshit…I'm a fuck with you bro.", Lightbulb pleaded his case.

"I'm your main man right. Who you call for to do this party?"

"Whatever man", Meechie chuckled then continued.

"Do yo thang Lightbulb, but you know I got you whenever you're ready to pop this shit off and make some real cash.

I only fucks with real niggas and your the realest they come.

I got nothing but love and respect for you bro.

You're the original go getter. Love!

Oh and by the way Redbone got off on that footwork. I know she won that 150."

"Yeah I got you Meech." Meechie and Lightbulb slapped hands giving each other a pound hug.

"Damn these young hoes in here fine as hell in here.

you know you be looking nigga!", Meechie said to Lightbulb before he and black walked back into the crowd, he turned and said to Lightbulb.

D.J. Lightbulb laughed, but seriously couldn't believe Meechie thought he was interested in those little ass girls.

"Let's go to the Mo...What?...Let's go to the Mo...What?...Let's go to the Mo...What?", the music played, while D.J. Lightbulb put back on his AKG K81 top of the line D.J. headphones then ending the mix.

«What›s good What›s good.

I'm ready to announce tonight's winner. The dancer who gets the loudest cheers wins $150.00."

Among all the dancers, Lemon and Big Ted received the loudest cheers. Although cheers were slightly louder when D.J. Lightbulb said Big Ted's name, Lemon won the $150.00. A few of the L.O.A girls rival dance crews booed her.

"I wish LiL Bit was here. She'll burn all these hoes up in juking.

She got raw footwork—that bitch is the truth.", one girl said to another girl in the crowd.

Shortly after Lightbulb announced Lemon as the winner,

people began to leave the boys and girls club.

Reflecting upon the hard work he has ahead of him to make the biggest juke show in Chicago happen, for a minute Lightbulb actually considered taking Meechie up on his offer as he loaded records into a milk crate. About 2:30 a.m., the Boys and Girls club auditorium was empty with just a few kids hanging around.

Lemon and her friend Auriel was last seen getting into Meechie's Charger. D.J. Lightbulb loaded all his equiptment into his Chevy Tahoe truck then drove away.

Meechie had hired some overnight janitors to clean the auditorium. It was hard to imagine just 20 minutes ago, the silent Boys and Girls auditorium was filled with loud juke music and screaming teenagers. While all that was going on the best juke dancer in Chicago was sleeping peacefully cuddled up with the teddy bear her deceased dad had given her.

Chapter 3

It was a beautiful saturday morning right after sunrise. The temperature was expected to reach a high of 85 degrees. It was either the smell of bacon, pancakes, grits, cheese eggs or the muffled sound of Mary J. Blige's song "Not Gon Cry!" blasting from the stereo in her living room that woke Lil Bit up out of her sleep.

Frustrated, Lil Bit climbed out of bed. She didn't have nothing against Mary J Blige, in fact she loved her music because of her mom, but waking her up to her out of her sleep was a different story. Lil Bit was heated. Making breakfast and singing loud as hell, Marose aggravated the shit out of Lil Bit.

"I'm not gon cry, I'm not gon cry, I'm not gon shed no tears No, I'm not gon cry, it's not the time cuz you're not worth my tears.", Marose sings happily.

Off balanced and still half asleep, Lil Bit stumped into the dining room. "MOM COULD YOU QUIET DOWN PLEASE...DANG!"

With a huge smile on her face and getting into the song, Marose spun around singing, despite Lil Bit's frustrated request.

"I was your lover and your secretary.

Working every day of the week.

Was at the job when no one else was there.

Helping you get on your feet."

Eleven years of sacrifice. And you can leave me at the drop of dime. Swallowed my fears, stood by your side I shoulda left your ass a thousand times. I'm not gon cry Heyy!", Marose sings playfully with all her soul over reacting getting into Lil Bit's face.

"MOM WHY YOU GOTTA BE SO LOUD.", Lil Bit complained moving her face away from her mom.

"You need to quit girl. Don't be waking up with no attitude.

It's my day off. I'm happy and I'm cooking for my kids. This is my house. Last I check.", Marose snapped turning down the stereo.

"But Mom why you gotta be so loud though, you woke me up!"

"Oh I'm sorry Lil Bit for waking you up in my house that I pay all the damn bills in, I'm so sorry baby.",

Marose said with a sarcastic laugh. Standing an inch shorter than Lil Bit, Marose was only 5 feet 2 inches tall. She was a smooth, light skinned cutie with cheeky, gorgeous sparkling brown eyes. She had cheek bones like a model's, and her lips were full and bright. She looked more like she could be Lil Bit's 22-year-old older sister than her 33-year-old mom.

"Mom Why you gotta get smart. and why you gotta be so loud daaanng!"

"Girl you know I love my Mary J. and it's the same reason you play that damn D.J. Flashlight juke twerk music all day and all night in my house Ms. Thang.", Marose said snapping her fingers acting goofy prolonging her playful mood aggravating Lil Bit even more than ever.

"It's D.J. Lightbulb.", Lil Bit said folding her arms.

"Forget it mom."

"Lightbulb Flashlight stoplight! Whatever the hell his name is. I know his mama gave him a real name", Marose laughed.

At this point in her life, Lil Bit and Savion was all Marose had. After spending 5 emotionally and physically abusive years with Savion's dad, she lost trust in men. And Marose truly never overcame her first love Lil Bit's Dad Jon Jon's murder. It seemed like it just happened yesterday, the pain of Jon Jon's murder was so vivid in Marose's mind.

From the first day Marose's mom met Jon Jon she loved him, but Mr. Williams wasn't as accepting of him. What father you know would actually like a boy who got his teenage daughter pregnant? However, the Williams grew to love Jon Jon; especially after he decided to post pone his first year of college on a Basketball Scholarship to spend time with his daughter. For Jon Jon it was a no brainer, he loved Marose and his daughter Lil Bit so much, he couldn't have imagined any other option but to stay home with them.

In fact, he gave Shatanya her nickname "Lil Bit", because she was a little itty bitty baby. He even made a song for Lil Bit's name that irritated the hell out of Marose because he would sing it so much. He would sing that song for hours throughout the day holding his baby girl.

"My Lil Bit...look at my Lil Bit...my little...itty...bitty...pretty...lil Bit...

my pretty daughter...and her pretty hair...she will always have my giant heart to share...look at my Lil Bit. look at my Lil Bit" And when Lil Bit was fussy and whiny, the itty bitty Lil Bit song was the only thing that would put her to sleep.

Marose begged Jon Jon to follow his dream and go straight to college and that they'll get married after he graduate from college and go into the N.B.A. Even Mr. Williams encouraged Jon Jon to go to school and not to pass up his basketball scholarship.

But Jon Jon's mind was made up, he wanted to stay at least the first year of Lil Bit's life. But on October 21st, 1992, was the worst day of Marose's life. Jon Jon's young life was taken and Marose's dream was shattered like a glass hitting the concrete. That morning Marose snapped cute pictures of Jon Jon with his long arms wrapped around Baby Lil Bit as they both slept peacefully. She had no warning no clue or no idea that would be the last picture she took of her first love and father of her child.

"Wake up baby!", Marose said kissing him snapping pictures. After each long kiss Marose whispered.

"Come on wake up baby!" Shifting his body, Jon Jon smiled enjoying Marose's kisses.

"Now that's the way a nigga suppose to wake up.",

Jon Jon said smiling.

"You trying to get something started girl."

"I don't care. Shatanya is sleep.", Marose replied.

Easing his arm from around Lil Bit trying not to wake her, Jon Jon pulled Marose on top of him gripping her ass." Then suddenly right before they were about to get it on. Lil Bit woke up.

"Waa...Waa...Waa!", Lil Bit cried.

Disappointed, Marose got up off Jon Jon then picked Lil Bit up.

"Lil girl—that's my man too", Marose laughed cradling Lil Bit before kissing her.

"You got us fighting over you boy!", Marose looked at Jon Jon.

"Look how good I look all the girls fight over me"

"Shut up Boy!", Marose snapped. After Jon Jon spent all morning with Marose and his daughter watching children learning shows, three of his friends came to get him to go shoot some basketball at the local gymnasium. Jon Jon put on his favorite Jordan Bulls Jersey and shorts, laced up his size 14 Jordans then picked up Lil Bit.

"Ooh ooh…wait Baby…let me take a picture of you and your favorite jersey holding Lil Bit."

"Come on Marose. I gotta go your always taking pictures.", Jon Jon complained.

"Baby you're so fine just this one time.", Marose said snapping their picture "ooh now kiss Lil Bit",

"You're tripping I gotta go girl"

"Just do it come on Jon Jon kiss Lil Bit."

"Can I go now!", Jon Jon said after kissing his daughter.

"Nope where's my kiss" Still holding Lil Bit in his arms, Jon Jon bent over and planted a sweet tongue kiss in Marose's mouth."

"Ok babe see you later—I gotta go love you."

"I love you too Jon Jon"

"Y'all nasty.",One of Jon Jon's homeboy said jokingly.

"Stop hating nigga! I can't help it you don't got no girl.", Jon Jon shot back.

"Whatever nigga just bring your ass and get dunked on."

The four young men started on their mile walk to the gym. It was a normal fall afternoon. People were out doing their thing. Running down the block, the boys were taking turns bouncing the ball and passing it to one another. Then out of no where a block away from the gym, 15 to 20 shots rang out. The boys got caught in the middle of cross fire between two rival gangs. The boys ran, but Jon Jon collapsed after only running a few yards. The gun men fled on foot. Realizing Jon Jon wasn't running with them, all 3 of his friends ran back to him laying on the ground gasping for air, bleeding from the neck and chess. In the blink of an eye, a peaceful fall day turned into a chaotic nightmare. People from the neighborhood were on their phones coming to Jon Jon's aid while some were shouting and cussing angry and fed up with the shootings in their neighborhood. Realizing it was him, friends from Jon Jon's block ran to him hollering for help.

"They always shooting around here, when will this BULLSHIT STOP", one lady hollered out. Cradling him in his arms, Jon Jon's friend Antwan begged and pleaded with him to fight for his life.

"Come on bro keep breathing bro, your gonna be alright.

You're gonna make it bro." Blood and tears were coming from Jon Jon's eyes. Face full of agony fighting for his life, Jon Jon cried.

"Lil Bit", He said gasping for air. Antwan couldn't make out his friends dying words.

"Lil Bit", Jon Jon cried again.

"Lil Bit she's going to be ok just keep breathing man."

"Tell Marose I love her", Jon Jon said before he took his last breath.

"No!", Antwan cried.

"Fuck No! come on man come on Jon Jon wake up man.

Where's the fucking ambulance!", Antwan cried. When the fire trucks, police and the ambulance arrived. Immediately they went to Jon Jon's aid, miraculously reviving him, but unfortunately Jon Jon died on his way to the hospital.

Meanwhile, back home Marose fed her baby Lil Bit, gave her a bath, did her hair and had dressed her up in the cutest little yellow and blue outfit. Lil Bit was as cute as a button with her chubby baby face. It had been 4 hours since Jon Jon left and Marose was expecting him to come walking thru the door any second.

She had made Taco's and was looking for to spending the weekend at home with him. Instead of the familiar sound of his keys rattling at the door, there was a stern knock at the door.

"That boy is so forgetful I hope he didn't lose his keys.", Marose thought to herself as she went to answer the door. Upon opening the door, she was confused and slightly worried to see two police officers and three of Jon Jon's friends.

"Where's Jon Jon?", She asked. Eyes watering and shaking his head, one of Jon Jon's looked down.

"Mam may we come in?",The bigger of the two officers asked. Immediately Marose begin to worry.

"Twan where's Jon Jon is he in jail what did he do?" Antwan was unable to look Marose in her eyes, at the point she knew something was wrong.

"He can't be in jail Jon Jon don't do nothing to nobody.", Marose said voice cracking with worry and nervousness.

"May we come in?" Letting them in, Marose closely examined Jon Jon friends faces.

"Mam there's no easy way of saying this and I'm very sorry. Jon Jon was an innocent bystander of a shooting. He was killed this afternoon."

"What?", She asked in disbelief not even trying to comprehend what the officer just told her.The policeman didn't bother to repeat those devastating words.

"Sorry mam"

"Oh my God...oh no!", Marose cried.

"Noooo!!", She screamed waking Lil Bit up. Her heart felt like it was about to burst. Like a glass hitting concrete her soul was shattered.

Looking at all the strange men in their home and her mom crying and screaming hysterically, was too much for Lil Bit's infant mind to process. Crying and screaming, Lil Bit looked up at them.

Jon Jon's friend Tone, immediately picked Lil Bit up trying his best to comfort her.

"No GOD NO...NO NO NO NO...OH GOD PLEASE NO HELP ME LORD.", Marose cried and screaming uncontrollably.

"Here's my card mam we're going to do everything in our power to catch the people who is behind this, we're gonna do a full investigation.

I'm so sorry for your lost.", The officer said before he and the other officer left Marose's apartment. Jon Jon's friends stayed with Marose and Lil Bit. It wasn't until an hour had passed before Marose could calm down. In an instance her world came to an end. Her body was numb. She didn't know what to do? Neither of Jon Jon's friends could find any words to say to help comfor Marose except hug her and say they were so sorry and if it there was anything she and Lil Bit needed they were always going to be there for them. They were just as in much pain and shock as Marose was about the death of their friend Jon Jon. They grew up with Jon Jon and had known him since the first grade.

News had got out about Jon Jon's death. Later that day—Marose's parents, Jon Jon's parent's, family and friends packed Marose's and Jon Jon's apartment. Later that night, they had to go identify the body.

At only 18 yrs old, It was the worst day of Marose's life.

Now 15 years later, at 33 years old, Marose was a struggling single mother of two, something she had never planned or imagined her life to be. But sometimes life has its way of going in the direction it wants to go in. Despite the negative affect Jon Jon's death had on her life, she survived and moved on. She was doing ok. She was as beautiful as ever, her looks sure hadn't changed in 15 years. She had a roof over her head—a nice car and working two jobs. She was doing ok.

Seated at the dining room table eating breakfast, Marose, Savion, and Lil Bit chatted... "What time did you get in last night girl?"

"I don't know mom maybe 12 or 1"

"12 or 1 Lil Bit!", Marose snapped. How many times I gotta tell you Shatanya. You're not grown girl. You're only 16 years old. You're a child. I can get in trouble for that."

"Stop tripping mom. I was with Katherine."

"I don't care who you was with. Don't come in my house after curfew. And besides why are you out that late with Katherine?"

"Ask her", Lil Bit snapped storming away from the dining room table.

"Bring your ass back here. What did I tell you about that disrespectful shit was wrong with you." Halfway to her room Lil Bit stopped. Turned around then walked back to the table. Arms folded she rolled her eyes looking at her mom with an attitude so sharp she could cut the tension with a knife.

"What's wrong with you Lil Bit?", Marose asked sympathetically.

"Nothing mom!", Marose said looking at Lil bit's stomach.

"Are you pregnant?"

"No mom, I'm not pregnant."

"Well what's wrong with you?"

"Nothing"

"Lord!", Marose said throwing her arms up looking up at the ceiling. "Oh John John, I need your help baby!" Marose complained.

"Didn't I tell you that you can talk to me about any and everything GIRL!"

"Yes Mom, but ain't nothing wrong with me, how many times I gotta to tell you that."

"If you ain't your daddy's lil girl, you act just like that man.

I hate when you act like him, burying your emotions...being stubborn as hell. I hate that shit Shatanya!" Again, Marose looked up to the heavens.

"JOHN JOHN...LORD KNOWS I NEED YOU BABY!"

"Why are you calling for him,.My daddy's dead and he's never coming back. You're always working. I don't got nobody, but that's alright though. I'm a survivor, I can take care of myself. This is my life!", Lil Bit snapped, shocking the hell out of Marose as Marose tried to figure out where all that came from.

"Is that what it's all about. You miss your daddy."

Tears began to form in Marose's eyes.

"I miss him too Lil Bit, I miss him so much, God knows how much I miss him. Somedays I can't go on without him. And don't ever say you don't got nobody, because you got me, your grandparents, and your Auntie Katherine."

"Uggh!", Lil Bit sighed at the sound of Katherine's name. With tears running down her face, Marose walked over to Lil Bit, putting her hands on her Lil Bit's arms.

"Look at you. Look at my beautiful daughter, all big and grown up. Man time flies by. I Love you so much Shatanya. I love you more than life itself. You're my lil girl; And if there's anything going on with you or if someone is bothering you. I need to know baby." Marose said feeling so bad for Lil Bit that she didn't enjoy the benefits of growing up with a dad like she did. Marose understood how important it was for a girl to have her dad in her life. Mr. Williams was the best dad any girl can ask for in Marose's eyes. He took care of his family very well.

"Mom! There's nothing wrong with me ok. Don't cry mom. I hate when you cry it makes me cry", Lil Bit replied turning her head away holding back tears of her own.

"I love you", Marose said hugging her daughter.

"I love you to Mom", Lil Bit said kissing Marose on her cheek as she walked to her room to get ready to go outside.

Although, throughout the years Marose tried keeping it all together, deep inside she was a wreck. In her lifetime, she experienced episodes of depression, anxiety, uncontrolled emotions, and even suicidal thoughts, after Jon Jon's murder. Walking back into the living room, she took a seat at the end of the couch.Crying and weeping, she laid her head on the arm of the couch.

"Mom stop crying!", Lil Bit said as she walked back into the living room giving her mom a hug. You always tell me to never let a person ruin my day, so don't let me ruin your day."

"You could never ruin my day Lil Bit.", Marose explained.

"I miss your daddy too; He would have been a good daddy to you, that man was so good. Oh I miss him so much.", Marose cried.

"Mom everything's gonna be alright. You are the best mom in the world and I wouldn't be this fine and sexy if it wasn't for you."

If it was one thing Lil Bit knew that would cheer her mom up was a compliment. Marose loved her some compliments.

"Girl you know you fine.", Lil Bit smiled causing Marose to low key blush.

"I can't believe you was listening to Mary J. Blige. I'm not gon cry and now you're up here crying." Pressing play on the stereo, Lil Bit turned up the volume a little...

"I'm about to play your song Mom. I know your bout to turn up now", Lil Bit laughed. Lil Bit had a way of brightening up Marose's day. Marose tried her best to fight her joyful emotions, but gave in to it, when her song came on grinning from ear to ear.

"Mom promise me your gonna be ok!" Rosey red cheeks, damped face from tears, sniffling. Marose smiled.

"I promise".

"Ok, I love you mom. I'll see you later."

"I love you to.", Marose waved goodbye as Lil Bit left their apartment.

Chapter 4

A mile away from Lil Bit's apartment building—the Ladies of Action dance group: Sway and Auriel were at Lemon's apartment listening to Juke music gossiping about niggas and bitches they knew from around their hood. Lemon's 9 year old sister Aniya and her gay boy cousin T.T was also hanging out with them in her apartment. Approaching the afternoon, the temperature was rising. It was hot out. The sun was shining bright. The girls were smoking weed. They had become bored and restless, so they decided to go outside and juke within the apartment's courtyard.

Living up to their crazy, sexy, and cool style, the girls were all about having fun, dressing sexy and having swag. They were like the hood version of the 90's group TLC. They were only teenager, ages 17 thru 19. They were about that life. Living the fast life in the streets of Chicago had matured the girls way beyond their teenage years.

"T.T help me put these speakers in the window" Lemon said passing the loud blunt to Sway.

"Bitch do I look like your maid.", T.T laughed snapping his fingers rolling his neck, eyes and hips like a little girl.

"T.T if you don't help me with these speakers nigga!", Lemon snapped back.

Lemon was the leader of the group. Lemon's grandmother nicknamed her Lemon because her bright light yellow skin complexion like a lemon. Her babyface was round like a young child. Those gorgeous almond dark brown eyes, full luscious lips, and her shapely body definitely turn heads.

Competitive, and bossy, Lemon was the dominant one of the group. Although, she wasn't the best juke dancer in the world, her confidence, sexiness, style, and bossy personality compensated for her wack ass juke dancing skills.

However, her girl Auriel was a beast juking, she was a much better dancer than Lemon and to throw gas on Lemon's flame's of jealousy, Auriel was much better looking with more ass to add to her sexiness.

Only thing imperfect about Auriel was that her teeth was slightly bucked, but her gleaming sparkling white teeth and beautiful smile had made it hard to notice. Auriel's butterscotch face was fresh, fine and healthy smooth like a baby's ass.

Her arched eyebrow's went perfectly with her gorgeous seductive eyes. The ridge of her cute nose between her nostrils was pierced with a thin solid gold hoop; her dark silky hair was pulled back into a ponytail.

Although Auriel and Lemon shared similar attributes, like sex appeal, style, and good looks, their personalities were like night and day. Lemon was aggressive, loud, sassy, stuck up, bossy, and manipulative.

Auriel was passive, naive, humble, submissive, and peaceful. Lemon had a habit of undermining whatever came out of Auriel's mouth. Ridicules and cruel insults from Lemon was the basis of their relationship, followed by apologies, such as.

"You know you my girl. I'm just trying to help you.", Lemon would always say. Stevie Wonder could see that Lemon was very insecure and jealous of Auriel. Sadly to say Auriel couldn't see through Lemon's insults, and came to the conclusion that Lemon could be a dirty bitch sometimes.

Even though Auriel was a beast juking, to keep things peaceful between her and Lemon, she'll let Lemon have the spotlight at dance wars. Don't get it twisted Lemon has some skills, but she couldn't fuck with Auriel. So Auriel dummied down her dance skills to make Lemon feel better about herself and to keep the peace between them.

Last but not least, the 3rd member of the trio dance group was Ms. Sway, short for Consuela, Sway was the wise, levelheaded, and mature girl of the group. She was a mixture of Lemon and Auriel all wrapped up in one, yet very wise. Sway was the heart, soul, and brains of the group. When Lemon gets besides herself being sadistic and callous towards Auriel, Sway would always jump in quickly defending Auriel putting Lemon in check.

Lemon knew better than to try Sway. Sway had a way of humbling Lemon's notorious heart. In fact Sway was the only one that would straight up tell Lemon that her Juking was weak as hell and she needs to practice more. And when Auriel acted passive and naïve, Sway encouraged her to stick up for herself and become more confident. To the girls, Sway was more of an older sister than a friend. She took no sides and showed no favoritism, Lemon and Auriel was her girls and she loved them both the same. Ladies of action for life was her motto.

Sway was 5"6" tall, dark skin and slightly overweight, but she wore her weight well. She was dark as night but she looked good for a big girl, she was absolutely beautiful, her face was exotic, she definitely had her share of admirers along with her sisters: Auriel and Lemon. Along with her beautiful looks, Sway never walked out of the house without being fresh and stylish. Even making a quick trip to the corner store, she had to look good. Bringing out her smooth chocolate black skin, she wore the best and more expensive weave then Gabriel Union, or any bitch off of Love and Hip Hop. As far as juking skills, she and Auriel ran neck to neck, it was hard to determine who was better. They were both a beast.

Each girl played their role well. Sway was the glue that kept them together. Lemon's sassy, sexy, and ruthless attitude gave their group their edge and infamous reputation. And Auriel super model video vixen good looks and super flawless juke moves attracted everybody. The Ladies of Action ran shit. It was times like this that the girls were at their best; getting along and having fun with one another practicing dance moves without any drama always strengthen their friendships. After Lemon and her gay cousin T.T put the speakers in the window. Lemon's 9 year old sister Aniya sat on the floor putting on her Nike's.

"Lemon can I come outside with y'all.", she asked.

"You gotta juke something sis!", Lemon said seriously.

"Ok...Ok.Ok", Aniya replied excitedly running and following behind Auriel, Sway, and T.T out of their mama 2nd floor apartment. Before, Lemon left out, she turned the volume up to its max then grabbed a few bottles of Gatorade, and orange pops. She ran downstairs to catch up with Aniya and them. Speakers in the window leaning on the screen, D.J. Lightbulb's new Juke mix download on Lemon's computer blasted echoing into the apartment's courtyard.

"Let me bang ♫♫♫ Let me bang ♫♫♫ Let me bang ♫♫♫ Let me bang ♫♫♫", The music played so loud that the noise could be heard a few blocks away. Outside along with a few neighborhood kids, Lemon, Sway, Auriel, T.T, and Aniya were now within the Apartment's courtyard. They were talking amongst each other deciding whether they should practice some moves and warm up or just dance. Within minutes, the loud juke music attracted a small crowd of neighborhood kids, teenagers, and even some adults.

"Let's just warm up and battle, we can practice some moves later", Lemon insisted. Posing and modeling Lemon began prepping up by shaking her legs and lifting her arms up parallel to her shoulders.

"1.2.3 Bang", Lemon said moving her feet and twisting her hips to the music.

"Let me bang ♫♫♫ Let me bang ♫♫♫ Let me bang ♫♫♫", The music played as Lemon seductively danced to the music. The D.J. Lightbulb mix switched to another song, the lyrics of the song mixed perfectly to the bass drum.

"Gone and drop it down ♫♫♫ Gone and drop it down ♫♫♫ Gone and drop it down ♫♫♫ Gone and drop it down" Watching Lemon dance, people began forming a circle around her nodding their heads.

Like Batman and Robin, Craig and Day Day, Kanye West and Jay Z, Flame and Yatta were best friends and inseperable. Bouncing their bodies, acting silly, they were watching from the crowd wanting to dance to. Everybody wanted to get their piece of the action. It was like the whole hood could footwork. In Chicago, Juke dancing was a sport. Both of the 18 years old boys stood tall and lanky, the innocent baby face looking boys were far from angelic. Sadly to say they were products of their environment, both involved in gangs, drugs, hustling, robbery and whatever it took to put money in their pockets they did it. They were a part of Meechie's infamous gang of thugs that controlled their east side Chicago neighborhood.

After Lemon concluded her dance routine, without hesitation like a young girl jumping double dutch, Auriel jumped in the dance circle.

"Bang bang bang skeet skeet skeet ♫♫♫ Bang bang bang skeet skeet skeet ♫♫♫ bang bang bang skeet skeet skeet"

Fiercely and swiftly moving her feet and body to the music, Auriel was the sexiest and best dance of the group.

"Bang bang bang skeet skeet skeet ♫♫♫ bang bang bang skeet skeet skeet ♫♫♫" Seeing sexy ass Auriel shake her booty and titties, without warning Yatta jumped in the circle playfully humping Auriel. She seemed not to mind as she stuck her big booty out shaking it like a salt shaker. Laughing and enjoying himself humping Auriel's booty like a cowboy, Yatta tapped out. Auriel feet were moving so fast, she made Yatta look bad.

Back at Lil Bit's crib, she was in a better mood ready to hit the streets. Although her spirits had been dampened for the past few weeks, today was a good day for her. She was able to talk to her mom over a bomb ass breakfast. Fresh out the shower and smelling good, her long curly hair was pinned back in a ponytail. A thin gold chain hung around her neck. And the fresh pair of new lady luck cool grey infrared Air Jordan 1 sneakers made her look fly and swaggerific. She had on a black seamless cami top that revealed her diamond pierced belly button. Wearing a pair of tight grey jogging pants hugging her round booty made her look fly and sexy.

"Where you going?", Marose asked.

"I don't know, probably by the school or over Dominique house. I'll be back later mom Love you.", Lil Bit said opening the front door.

"Love you too", Marose said watching Lil Bit leave their apartment.

Inhaling the fresh humid air, Lil Bit stepped out onto the sidewalk walking and looking to get into something. Not even, outside a good few minutes, dudes were already trying to holla—honking their horns at her acting thirsty. She became so use to it, she barely noticed the young man walking towards her from across the street.

"Aye baby What's your name.", he said passing by her. As usual she ignored the perverts, but this time she smiled at the young man because she thought he was cute. The further she walked down 74th street, the louder and clearer the music became.

Instead of walking to the spot where her friends were at, she followed her ears down 75th street. The crowd of people she saw and the juke music blasting caught her attention as she headed towards the party.

"Lets go to the moe! What? ♫♫♫ Let's go the moe! What? ♫♫♫ Let's go the moe! What?", Lyrics from the song echoed in the neighborhood.

Squinting her eyes nodding her head, Lil Bit smiled.

"Ohhh shit!", She said to herself bawled fist covering her mouth as she approached the crowd of cheering teens watching Sway footwork.

Lil Bit's friend 11 year old sister Melissa noticed her. Melissa loved, idolized, and worshiped Lil Bit because of her style, good looks, and talented footworking.

Fuck Rhianna' this little girl wanted to be like Lil Bit.

"Lil Bit!", Little Melissa hollered running towards Lil Bit.

"They juking", Little Melissa said excited and bugged eyed, pulling on Lil Bit's arm.

"Dang girl Calm down!", Lil Bit chuckled.

"Oh Shit it's Lil Bit", a teenage boy said also frantic, excited and bugged eyed.

It wasn't long before a few other kids and teenagers from the hood noticed she was there. They were all saying the same thing.

"Juke something Lil Bit" or "Are you gonna Juke?"

Soaking up every moment of their praises and attention, Lil Bit felt like a star. She couldn't help but blush yet she remained calm, cool, and collected. She sported a mean poker face.

"I'm thinking about it.", She finally answered with a sly smile nodding her head to the music looking at Sway juke.

"Who's that?", Lil Bit asked.

"That's Sway, she's with Lemon and them. You've heard of L.O.A?", One of the neighborhood guys asked...

"L.O.A?"

"Yeah Ladies of Action click some shit like that, they a lil dance group.", The boy replied. "But you know they can't fuck with you."

Jumping up and down Little Melissa got in Lil Bit's face frantically pulling her arm.

"Please Juke Lil Bit. I love when you Juke.", Little Melissa begged.

"I'm gonna juke Melissa. please.stop pulling on my arm girl.", Lil Bit laughed nodding her head to the music.

"Let me bang ♫♫♫ Let me bang ♫♫♫ Let me bang ♫♫♫ Let me bang.", the music played.

Using one of their moves the girls practiced time and time again to perfection, striking a pose signaling Lemon to start Juking, Sway and Lemon slid past each other: as Sway exited the juke circle while Lemon entered the Juke circle.

Sloppily Juking like an amateur, nobody couldn't tell Lemon that she wasn't the shit; even though some of her moves were nice and others were horrible as a white girl trying to twerk, Lemon went in with more confidence then Lebron James slam dunking the ball through the rim in a NBA title playoff game.

Like an American Idol contestant, **thinking** she has a voice like Whitney Houston but really has no talent embarrassing herself, Lemon danced like M.C. Hammer couldn't touch this. If Lemon wasn't so much in her zone and paying attention, she would have seen the frowns on people's faces and hear the giggles and laughter coming from the crowd at how stupid she looked.

"WHO is That!", Lil Bit asked with a disgusted frown on her face.

"Lemon!", a girl in the crowd replied.

"Who told her she can footwork.", Lil Bit laughed.

"Let me bang ♫♫♫ let me bang ♫♫♫ let me bang", **the music played.**

Moving closer to the center of the crowd facing the dance circle, preparing for battle nodding her head to the music, Lil Bit's entire demeanor changed. Her muscles tensed up and her heart rate increased. Lil Bit's facial features were so innocent, angelic and beautiful, she couldn't look threatening if she wanted to. Nevertheless, she was in her zone, her eyebrows were pulled down together, glaring open like a battle rapper in a freestyle battle, Lil Bit mean mugged Lemon.

"Let me bang ♫♫♫ Let me bang ♫♫♫",The music blasted.

The temperature was rising and it was getting hotter. The sun was out and the whole hood was out there enjoying the juke battle. No fighting and no shooting, everyone was enjoying the dance contest.

"Bitch!", Lemon whispered to herself rolling her eyes and neck, after she noticed Lil Bit mean mugging her. Anticipating her first move, the kids and teenagers, who knew Lil Bit and saw her Juke before looked excited. They couldn't wait to see her in action.

"Let me bang ♫♫♫ Let me bang ♫♫♫", The repetitive lyrics blended with an 808 kick drum. Added with the sound when Ms. Pac man eats the dots and when one of the ghost kills Pac man mixed back and forth banging loud from the speakers in Lemon's window. "♫♫♫ ♫♫♫ ♫♫♫ ♫♫♫ ♫♫♫ ♫♫♫ (Ms Pac man music)."

"Go Lil Bit...Go Lil Bit Go Lil Bit...Go Lil Bit", Little Melissa and her friends cheered for her.

Looking at Lil Melissa, Lil Bit smiled.

They ain't ready for me, she thought to herself. Not only was Lil Bit an awesome Juke and Twerk Queen, she knew how to build up anticipation and get the crowd into it cheering her on, begging her to Juke, Sway and Auriel were wondering who the fuck she was. And why was everybody so super geeked about this short Ashley Banks from Fresh prince of Bel-air look-a-like. Of course they seen her in school and around the hood for many years, but they didn't know she juked. And now they were about to find out about the hoods best kept secret that's if only Lemon would ever get her wack ass from out of the Juke circle. But Lemon being Lemon she had to soak up all the spotlight she could get. Waving her arms like a retard, causing Lil Bit to slightly flinch, Lemon danced her way smack dead in front of Lil Bit's face causing Lil Bit to slightly flinch.

Nevertheless, Lil Bit was the least affected by whatever the hell Lemon was doing. If she was trying to intimidate Lil Bit it wasn't working. Lil Bit laughed at her.

"You can't fuck with me Bitch!", Lemon said whipping her hair back then walked away.

"What BITCH?", I'm the Floyd Mayweather of this shit HOE!", Lil Bit snapped. The bass dropped in the music. Then what appeared to be in slow motion, Lil Bit's body went to the right. The 808 bass drum dropped again. Then her body went to the left. Like a target she was on point. She didn't miss a beat. The mix switched up and played back to its original speed. "Fuck it!", Lil Bit said smiling with excitement because it was by the grace of God that her favorite mix was playing.

"Get down Lil mama! ♫♫♫ Get down Lil mama! ♫♫♫ Get down Lil mama!♫♫♫ Get down Lil mama! ♫♫♫"

Lil Bit took off faster than an airplane on the run way. Never missing a beat, at the speed of light, her brand new lady luck cool grey infrared jordans dribbled quickly as her body and booty bounced to the beat.

"Get down Lil mama! ♫♫♫ Get down Lil mama! ♫♫♫ Get down Lil mama! ♫♫♫ Get down Lil mama! ♫♫♫", the music played.

Suprisingly Lil Bit was slightly off beat, not because she couldn't dance. That was like saying Jennifer Hudson couldn't sing. No, but because her feet was moving a ½ second faster than the 190 bpm up tempo melody and beat she was juking to. As Lil Bit juked her ass off, some people in the crowd stared in awe and disbelief. Others went insane excitingly cheering Lil Bit on. Excited, one boy hollered.

"Lil Bit's the truth!. Lil Bit's truth", The young spectator hollered jumping up and down twirling in a circle unable to keep his composure. For some odd reason, Lil Bit's juking had that effect on people.

Even Sway, Auriel, T.T, and Lemon's baby sister Aniya stared in awe at LilBit's electrifying performance. They couldn't believe what they were watching.

"That bitch got heat", Sway whispered to Auriel staring at Lil Bit in disbelief.

"Get down Lil mama! ♫♫♫ Get down Lil mama! ♫♫♫,"

Seductively rubbing her titties, ass, and pussy, Lil Bit got sexy on them.

She got down on all fours and bounced her booty in every direction— east, west, south, and north.

Eyebrows curled downward, lips poked out, blood boiling with hatred and jealousy, Lemon was unable to hide her frustration. She was salty. She was embarrassed.

Lil Bit went in for the kill, her feet went into torque speed, disrespecting Lemon in her face with every dance move making Lemon the shadow of shame for the day. Lil Bit went crazy flexing her body like a rubber band. She was humiliating Lemon so bad that Sway and Auriel had to jump in running to Lemon's defense. Flame jumped into the battle circle swooping Lil Bit off her feet.

"Slow down slow down shorty, You won!," Flame said trying to calm Lil Bit down walking her away to the street.

"I'M THE FLOYD MAYWEATHER OF THIS SHIT BITCH! UNDERSTAND ME," Lil Bit hollered.

Although Lil Bit was slightly exhausted from dancing her adrenaline and emotions kept her yelling obsentities at Lemon. Walking Lil Bit down the block, Flame tried calming her down.Tired and exhausted, she collapsed in Flame's arms.

"Can I have that", Lil Bit said pointing at the bottle water in Flames pocket.

Flame gave her the water. "You be snapping shorty.", Flame laughed... "you good?", he asked.

The sweat on Lil Bit's smooth caramel brown face made her baby hairs from her head stick to her forehead.

"I just love juking", Lil Bit explained as they walked back to the apartment's courtyard to check out the other dancers.

When they noticed Flame and Lil Bit coming back to the courtyard, the kids began to cheer for her while others teased Lemon for losing.

"She got in your ass Lemon.", one of the bad ass neighborhood kids laughed, teasing Lemon then running away.

Walking along side of Lil Bit, Flame looked down at her.

"I ain't never seen nobody Juke like that shawrty, you killed everybody out there."

"Thanks!", Lil Bit smiled as she admired Flame's cute boy features face and Long slender body.

Sway walked over a few yards to where Flame and Lil Bit were chatting.

"Hey Girl! I've been seeing you in school and around the hood for years. I didn't know you could juke like that. Girrll you got heat!"

"Thanks!", Lil Bit replied.

From a distance Lemon and Auriel stared at Lil Bit with mean hateful looks on their faces.

"Come on girl!", Lemon said to Auriel marching over to where Flame, Lil Bit, and Sway were standing and talking with each other.

"BITCH WHY WAS YOU ALL IN MY FACE HOE, HUH BITCH", Lemon hollered trying to run up on Lil Bit.

"YOU THINK YOUR HAIR IS ALL CUTE AND LONG I'M ABOUT TO RIP THAT SHIT OUT BITCH YOU SHOULDN'T HAVE BEEN TALKING SHIT!!", Lemon snapped.

In an instance Sway and Flame jumped in front of Lemon as Lil Bit backed up throwing her fist up like Floyd Mayweather.

"WHAT RATCHET UGLY BITCH YOU AIN'T GONNA PULL SHIT OUT HOE!! COME ON!", Lil Bit screamed pushing Flame in his back, trying to get at Lemon and keeping her in eyesight.

Flame threw his long arms up towering over the girls.

"CHILL THE FUCK OUT Y'ALL ITS JUST JUKING!", Flame hollered trying to de-escalate the situation.

"Let her Go! SO SHE CAN GET FUCKED UP!", Lil Bit hollered ready to fight. Standing her ground with her fist up, patiently waiting on the first bitch to get in her face, so she can swing and knock the first bitch out that gets in her face.

"Stop Girl, it's just juking!", Sway said grabbing Lemon.

"MOVE SWAY!", Lemon snapped in a threatening tone.

Watching the fight, the crowd moved towards the sidewalk where all the commotion was happening as the music continue to play. The block was rowdy and ghetto as hell as kids instigated for them to fight.

"Lil Bit's gonna beat your ass Lemon!", someone hollered from the crowd. "CHILL OUT Y'ALL CHILL OUT Y'ALL", Flame hollered as he fought with Lemon and Auriel trying his best to hold them back.

Now in the street, Lil Bit backed up. Then all of a sudden, Lemon looked ill, she began to feel bile filling her mouth.

The crowd of kids parted like the red sea when Lemon bent over holding her stomach and start vomiting.

In an instance the crowd, Sway, and Flame went from going against Lemon to showing her compassion and support. Sway sympathetically guided Lemon to the closest tree, where she puked three more times on the tree.

For support, Lemon put her right hand on the tree then puked for the 4th time.

Her morning breakfast was splattered all over the tree, grass, and side walk.

"Lemon, you're alright?", Auriel panicked. Although, Lil Bit brow frowned, eyes darting about in concern at the sight of Lemon puking, she still couldn't help telling herself.

"That's what you get bitch!"

Helping her stand up from the slouched over position she was in, Auriel and Lemon's gay cousin T.T helped her walk back to her apartment building.

"You alright Girl! We gonna get you in the house.", T.T said in his best gay concerned voice with his arms around his favorite cousin.

Disbelief seized them all, after they took Lemon home. Even Lil Bit couldn't make sense of what just happened. All Lil Bit remembers was blacking out going into her dance zone. Next, a bitch wanted to fight her, then the bitch start throwing up.

What the fuck? Shit's crazy, Lil Bit thought to herself.

With her arm around Lemon's baby sister Aniya, Sway shook her head, looking at Lil Bit.

"I'm sorry girl, that bitch got problems, that's my bitch and I love Lemon to death, but she gotta real fucked up attitude. Somebody's gonna beat her ass one of these days.", Sway explained as Lemon's baby sister Aniya stared at Lil Bit with contempt. Little Aniya's feelings about Lil Bit was in conflict, she was amazed and flabbergasted on how amazing Lil Bit's juke dancing was, but at the same time—this bitch just got into it with my Big sister. Putting her little hand on her hip, Aniya mean mugged Lil Bit with a serious attitude.

She wasn't sure to defend her Big sister's honor and be mad at Lil Bit or get excited and hug and praise Lil Bit for that amazing juke performance.

"What's wrong with her?", Lil Bit asked Sway about Lemon.

"She's just ignorant as hell", Sway replied.

"No! I mean why was she throwing up everywhere."

"I don't know girl, to be truthful, I think that bitch is pregnant."

Glancing at Aniya, Lil Bit noticed how she was looking at her.

Remembering what her big sister had always told—"I don't care if I'm right or wrong, you're my sister and you're suppose to always have my back", Aniya remembered as she shifted her body.

"Hoe!", Aniya snapped rolling her eyes at Lil Bit.

"Go in the house girl!", Sway said shoving Aniya away.

"I'm telling my sister.", Aniya said walking away.

"I don't care tell her and get your ass in the house.", Sway demanded.

"You don't be calling nobody out there name."

Lil Bit was shocked at Aniya's comment, but she kept her composure understanding the fact that she was just a little girl.

Upstairs, T.T. turned the music off and took the speakers out of the window. The kids in the neighborhood began to go their separate ways, after the fight was over.

Flame and Sway stayed with Lil Bit and chatted with her for a few moments. Until Yatta walked up, sporting an intense expression on his face.

"We gotta go Fam...Meech just hit me up, he says it's important, we got nation business to handle."

"Alright, here I come fam", Flame replied as he turned at Sway.

"Aye Sway make sure Lemon and them don't fuck with her.", Flame said, before walking away with Yatta. Sway stayed with Lil Bit for the rest of the day. They talked and walked around the neighborhood. The more they talked, the more they discovered things they both had in common. Sway told Lil Bit about their dance group. Lil bit thought Sway was real cool. Before they went their separate ways, the girls exchanged numbers and promised to see each other and hang out again.

Chapter 5

The way Ricky in Boyz-n-the hood felt about Compton, when he and
Tre visited Tre's father at his job, was the same way Flame felt about
Englewood on the south side of Chicago. Watching his back at every
corner, Flame looked uncomfortable.

"Fuck Meechie doing over here for!", Flame frantically asked Yatta.

"Stop being a pussy Nigga!"

"Fuck you nigga!", Flame snapped back.

"I just don't fuck with Englewood like that, my cousin got killed over here."

"We got Banga, these niggas ain't on shit."

"Banga! A nine don't got shit on grenades, Cap 40's, Ak's, Assault Rifle's,
and Fast Mags."

"You play too much call of duty", Yatta replied shaking his head.
Flabbergasted, Yatta couldn't believe Flame was acting like a pussy.

"Scarry Ass! What did Furious Styles say from Boyz-n-the hood. It's 07
Flame don't be afraid of your own people.", Yatta laughed as he prepared to
park in front of a duplex at night in Englewood.

"Come on Fam!", Yatta said after he parked his car tucking a semiautomatic
firearm in the front of his waist, opening the car door then hopping out onto
the sidewalk. A few guys in the gangway and three hittas on the block had
been watching Yatta's car ever since they first bend a corner on their block.

"What's up G? Who y'all looking foe?", one of the hittas asked.

"Meechie!", Yatta answered with his chin up and chest out.

"Oh, y'all must be his folks, yeah he's up in there.", one of the hittas said
pointing at the house.

"Good looking fam!", Yatta thanked them as he made his way to the
dublex. Closely watching over his shoulder, Flame followed Yatta upstairs.

2 knocks pause then 7 rapid knocks is 27, backwards for 72. It stood for 72nd street—the block Flame, Yatta, and Meechie grew up on. Meechie opened the door.

"What up Boy?", Meechie greeted them letting them in.

"Come on in."

"I didn't know you fucks with Englewood.", Flame said to Meechie as they sat down.

"I'm worldwide baby", Meechie laughed.

The sound of grease popping came from the kitchen. The smell of fried pork chops, marijuana, and raspberry incense burning gave Meechie's first floor duplex apartment an unique aroma. A half naked thick thighs caramel skin woman walked out of the kitchen.

"Whose in my House?", the beautiful young lady in panties wearing a long blue bob marley shirt asked. Starring then quickly looking away—Flame and Yatta tried their best not to look at Meechies girl Big ass and thighs, but they couldn't help but steal a glace or two.

"Man I got company go put some fucking clothes on.", Meechie fussed.

"I didn't know Meechie damn!", the half naked video vixen look-a-like snapped back.

After they all sat down, Meechie passed Flame the lit backwoods.

"Aye, y'all nigga's ready to come the fuck up, I'm talking about racks over racks."

"Do shit stank! Hell yeah we ready to get that Gwop.", Flame laughed slapping hands with Yatta.

"Alright then niggas, check this out. I gotta sweet lick on this nigga named Poncho.

He lives out in the south suburbs.

This bitch ass nigga been owing me 5 racks for 6 months now.

This motherfucka done bought 2 bricks of raw and 3 pounds of loud from me since then, but this motherfucka can't give me my 5 racks, only reason I ain't been sweating his bitch ass cuz he's spending bread with me."

"Fuck that! I would've made that nigga pay me my money!", Yatta interrupted. "Fo Sho! But check this out I know all about this goofy, he's a dick rider; he wants to be like me.", Meechie laughed and continued.

"I know all about this motherfucka, he got about 50 racks maybe more in a safe in his room, he got 20 to 30 pounds of reggie in his garage, and in a room down stairs, he got hundreds of e pills and a pound or two of loud for all the bitches his trick ass be tricking with, so y'all wanna get this Fuck boy or What?"

"Hell Yeah!", Flame said excitedly then stood up.

"That motherfucka's good is got!", Yatta added amped up and smiling deviously.

"Well good, cuz it's going down tonight!"

"What's good then, we ready.", Yatta said spreading his arms.

Both Yatta and Flame were ready and hungrier than two blood thirsty pitbulls to rob Poncho.

"Calm down boy, you be beasting.", Meechie laughed.

"I gotta tell y'all the scoop, he lives with his girl and daughter."

"His daughter?", Flame said with concern.

"Yeah his daughter mothafucka! You gotta problem with that.", Meechie replied shaking his head.

After over a decade of friendship, Yatta and Flame looked at each other and sensed each other. A little girl at this nigga crib this might not be a good idea, they both thought to themselves. "Y'all gotta problem with that?", Meechie asked.

"Nah, it ain't a problem Meechie, right Flame.", Yatta said looking at flame hoping he ain't about to fuck up the opportunity.

"Yeah it ain't no problem fam!", Flame agreed hesitant to agree with Yatta.

"Alright then, this is a 100 G lick, I ain't with hurting nobody either, but y'all know the rules no witnesses, it's on y'all, but you don't wanna be sitting in jail for a motherfucker pointing you out or worst than that a nigga's catch you slipping and come back and wack yo dumb ass. Although, I seriously doubt it with Poncho's lame ass, but you can't underestimate no one.",

They shot at nigga's before, snatched a few purses, and even jumped some dudes. But, neither one of them never killed a person, not yet! Despite Flame's apprehensive expression on his face, Yatta was game to do whatever for the scrilla, gwop, cream, bread, racks or whatever name you want to call it, Yatta was down to do whatever for the money.

Killing a child was something he would never think of doing, especially with as many of his friend's in the hood younger siblings who were innocent victims that died from senseless gunfire. Yatta lost count from all the kids he knew 15 years and younger that was killed, but there was nothing he could do about their deaths, the damage was already done. And if it meant for him to get some money, he would do whatever?

"I gotsta get paid Chalie—So Whaddup?", Yatta said ready and willing to do their deadly deed. For Meechie, killing and robbing niggas was just another day at the office. Meechie's grin was more devious and devilish than the joker from batman.

"Be right back!", Meechie said.

After taking a few deep puffs from the blunt, Yatta looked at Flame.

"You looking like you don't want to get paid."

"It ain't that nigga! I ain't with running up on no little girls with banga's.", Flame said shaking his head.

"Maan! we ain't running up on no little girls with guns, we just stanging this nigga. We gonna whoop the nigga ass. Tie em up. Get all the Gwop, loud, and epills. Then we out that bitch." Yatta said shaking Flame's shoulder.

"We about to be stunting on nigga's, fucking all the bitches. This is our chance nigga!"

Carrying a big duffle bag, Meechie walked back into the living room dropping the bag and the shoe box on the couch.

"Ski masks and gloves!", Meechie smiled tossing the duffle bag on to the couch.

"That's what's up!", Yatta said grabbing the ski masks and gloves out the bag "Hell yeah those those real O.J. joints!", Meechie laughed.

"No doubt nigga!", Flame added.

"Y'all need missles right?", Meechie asked.

"Yeah! Hell yeah!", Yatta replied eagered to get his hands on another gun to add to his collection. Meechie handed Yatta a 380 automatic.

"That's what's up?", Yatta said admiring the gun before tucking it into the small of his back.

"So do dude got guns at his crib."

"Yeah, but it ain't nothing major tho! Maybe a shotgun or something, Y'awl good tho! Y'awl nigga's ain't new to this.", Meechie replied receiving the blunt from Yatta.

"Baa bee! You wanna hit this blunt.", Meechie hollered for his girl in the kitchen. "Put on some clothes before you bring yo ass out here to.", Meechie said puffing the blunt."

"You gotta keep these hoes in check, I don't need y'all thirsty ass niggas looking at my girl's ass and shit.", Meechie laughed.

Meechie took a few leaps to and from the kitchen back into the living room, after passing his girl the blunt. Short of breath, he sits down then leaned forward.

"Alright fella's—it's cracking tonight. This a big power move. a hunned g's worth!

Y'all my niggas and I want y'all to come up, so all I want is 10 g's for it. The other 90 racks is all y'awl money. I don't give a fuck what y'awl do with it, but you better help out y'awl mama's and don't trick it off. 90 or 80, but I know for a fact it's not gonna be less than 70 racks. It's gonna be 70 racks at the least, you can take his jewelry, guns, flat screens, clothes or whatever he got."

"I don't want the nigga clothes.", Flame interrupted with a laugh. The way Flame and Yatta were leaned in paying attention to Meechies instructions, you would think they were front row at an UFC fighters match.

Flame and Yatta followed Meechie into his bedroom.

"I didn't want my girl to hear me.", Meechie said closing the bedroom door.

"I went to the strip club with the nigga one night and we took some bitches to the hotel to bust down and shit like that, so I kept in touch with one of the bitches, and the bitch he was fucking with been telling me all about how he be tricking off on her, blowing ounces of loud with her, giving her E pills and shit. She been talking reckless about the nigga about how the nigga stank and he gotta little dick bullshit like that, I don't give a fuck about. But anyways she got zero respect for the nigga. So ole girl gonna set it up and hit him up tonight and buy 30 E pills from him—she got the trick nigga wrapped around her pussy. He does whatever the bitch tell him to do; but I kind of feel him though, the bitch is bad as hell and that head is bomb ass fuck.", Meechie said laughing, squeezing his eyes shut tight shaking his body with excitement from the thought of the few times he spent with that thot bitch, causing Flame and Yatta to laugh hysterically.

"I'm a ride out there with ya'wl. Show y'awl where he lives. All Y'awl gotta do is wait until he gets back home and get his ass. It's that simple."

"Bet!", Flame and Yatta responded simultaneously. Both goon faced. Do or die. No turning back. They were ready. Seriously down for committing their infamous assignment. Holding his chin up Yatta asked Flame.

"You ready to get paid nigga?"

"Hell Yeah!", Flame answered with a sinister tone in his voice completely indifferent from the moral goodness attitude he had 15 minutes ago, hesitant to rob a man with his young daughter in the house. That fast his mind set switched from Martin Luther King Jr. to Bin Laden. Flame looked at Meechie and Yatta with a serious expression.

"We gotta get paid fam! Let's hope his daughter ain't there."

"Don't worry If she's there we ain't gonna hurt no little girl.", Yatta reassured Flame.

"So shorty gonna call me when Poncho's on his way to meet her.", Meechie said shaking his head.

"All the nigga had to do was pay me my 5 racks. Dick riding faggot, trying to be like me. Now his ass is got", Meechie laughed, shaking up with Flame and Yatta as they went back into the living room.

A few hours had passed and they were wondering if the bitch was ever gonna call. Flame and Yatta was losing hope and growing restless, thinking they'll never ball out. Meechie was ready to tell them nigga's to leave his crib and get with his old stick up crew and rob the nigga himself.

Then Meechie's phone rings.

"Whaddup?", He answered. It was the call they had been waiting for, she filled Meechie in on everything about Poncho.

Excited and giggling with each other, Flame and Yatta threw on their black hoodies and scooped up their ski masks and gloves.

"Come on!", Meechie waved his hand, after he hung up with the bitch.

Meechie got in his car. Flame and Yatta jumped in theirs.

For 30 minutes, they followed Meechie out to Poncho's house in the suburbs. The time was 11:38 p.m., when Meechie stopped in the middle of a street in a neighborhood full of upscale suburban homes with Yatta in the car behind him.

Yatta phone rings!

"Yeah whaddup Meechie?"

"Aye follow me to the next block and come jump in my whip."

"Aight! Bring Heat?"

"Naw. Just follow me.", Meechie said pulling away as Yatta followed him from behind to the next block then parked his car.

Yatta hopped in front while Flame hopped in the backseat of Meechie's car.

"What's popping?", Yatta asked.

"Shit! I'm about to just show y'awl where he stay at?", Meechie said pulling off. Just a few blocks away from where Yatta was parked, Meechie points to a house.

The house was new. It looked like it had been finished last month. The light blue home had exhibited warmth and coziness in some way.

"That's his crib right there." Meechie said slowly rolling pass Poncho's house pointing at it for the second time.

"The one with that old ass motorcycle in the front.", Yatta asked paying close attention to his surroundings remembering exactly where Poncho's house was located—street name, neighbor's homes, cars, and all.

"Yelp!", Meechie replied. Flame was already thinking ahead.

"We can wait in them bushes by his garage."

"That's why you're my nigga. I was thinking the same thang.", Yatta replied seconding that motion.

"All I can say is just handle y'awl motherfucking business. This ain't no $700 or $800 stang fam. This some real gwop, so stay on yo! P's and Q's" Meechie explained as he drove back to the block where Yatta's car was parked.

"I hear you Meech.", Yatta said looking at Flame in the back seat.

"I gotta make sure my nigga is ready. You ready bro?"

"Stop asking dumb ass questions.", Flame said sporting a goon face.

"I hope so man, just stay focused. Get paid and be out.", Meechie said stopping besides Yatta's car.

"Come straight to my crib when y'awl done.",

"We got this Joe. We about this life.", Yatta said before he and Flame hopped out of Meechie's car and back into his whip, he started it up then drove off.

A few blocks away and a few minutes later, Yatta found a parking space a short distance away from Poncho's house. Putting on his gloves, Yatta turns to Flame.

"Bro we fenna just handle this shit! Straight like that You ready my nigga", he asked. Locked and loaded, the clicking and clacking of the metal made it official.

"Hell Yeah I'm ready!", Flame said with the 380 in his hand.

"Bet dat up, we just waiting on Meech's call!" Unknowingly and unaware of their future, the boys waited patiently for Meechie's call that could either ruin their young lives or give them temporary monetary satisfaction. Either way it turns out, their decision to rob and even kill a family for drugs and money was a lose/lose situation. After 15 minutes of waiting, Yatta phone ringtone rings playing a song by Lil Boosie.

"You don't know my struggle ♫♫♫ You can't knock my hustle ♫♫♫ You don't know what I been through." The song ended, when Yatta answered.

"Talk to me"

"What up Fam? It's on I just talk to ole girl, she said Poncho just left her hotel. Y'all ready?"

"Speak no moe Fam, We got this."

"Aight cool!", Meechie replied as he hung his phone up.

"That was Meechie. Come on!"

Each holding a gun, they tucked their weapons in the waist of their black jeans. In all black, black hoodies, black air force ones. With ski masks in hand, they hopped out of Yatta's vehicle disappearing into the dark night. Jogging between houses and bushes until they reached the side of Phoncho's garage, they put the ski masks on.

Carefully and quietly they stood between a huge tree with their backs against Poncho's garage.

"I saw some lights on.", Flame whispered.

"Yeah me to." Yatta said looking both ways.

"Somebody's in there. We gon wait till he pull up then rush him."

"Alright Cool!", Flame whispered.

Ten minutes had passed and still no sign of Poncho.

"Fuck this nigga at?", Yatta whispered.

"I don't know, but I'm ready to get the fuck out of here. I'm tired of waiting."

"I feel you fam. This nigga ain't coming man."

Right before the boys were about to jog back to Yatta's car, bright headlights illuminated the driveway, the low sound of Bass bumping came from a gray Chrysler 300 pulling into the driveway caught the boys attention. Stopping Flame, Yatta stretched his arm out.

"That's him!", Yatta whispered gripping the handle of his 9 millimeter glock from his waist slowly retrieving it. The only thing that coulb be heard was the sound of foot steps squishing in moist grass when Flame and Yatta took a few steps back to the side of the garage. They crept slow. Yatta peeped around the side of the garage then turns to Flame.

"Shhhh", He whispered. The music and bass from Poncho's car suddenly stopped. His driver's door was in need of motor oil, WD40, or Silicone spray because the door creaked very loudly when he opened it.

With Banga's drawn Yatta and Flame swooped from around the corner like Bat man and Robin, Billie the Kid and Jesse James. Before Poncho could fully get his large body out of his car with one foot on the ground, 2 guns were aimed at his head.

"Make one sound and we squeezing.", Yatta said meaning business.

"Whose in the house?"

"My family man my girl and my daughter, Y'awl want this car. Y'awl can have this car man", Poncho cried frightened half to death—shaking in his size 44 jeans. Flame's gun Clicked clacked when he cocked back the 380.

"Nigga you think we playing. Say something!", Yatta said grabbing Poncho by his shirt pressing the hole of the barrel of his 9 millimeter against Poncho's temple as he yanked him from the car.

"Open the garage faggot."

"Alright alright alright man", Poncho cried and pleaded, pondering the thought of who the fuck is these nigga's with ski masks on with guns pointed at his head, Poncho's life flashed before his eyes. They meant business and the best thing for him to do was do whatever they say.

The electronic noise of the garage door opening echoed inside Poncho's garage. With the gun still pressed against Poncho's head Yatta twisted the metal harder against Pocho's head.

"Come on Bitch!", Yatta said pushing Poncho forward. Flame grabbed the garage door opener and yanked Poncho's car keys from the ignition. Once he was inside, he closed the garage door with the remote then flicked on the light switch to the garage.

"Listen up motherfucka! If we get all what we came here for then we won't have to smoke you and them bitches in there you hear me!",

Flame said pointing his gun in Poncho's back.

"Alright man please man whatever you want my girl and my daughter in there, Please don't kill us!"

Holding guns at Poncho, one at his head, the other at his back. Yatta and Flame carefully walked him from the garage upstairs to a small hallway inside his house.

"Shut the fuck up.", Yatta whispered angrily with his finger on the trigger as he pushed Poncho upstairs causing Poncho to stumble.

Poncho's girl turned on the hallway light.

"Baby that's you?", She asked. At first glance of Poncho and the two ski masks gunmen behind him, for a split second she thought it was a fucked up way to try to play a joke on her. Then reality set in quickly. The look on Poncho's face was no laughing matter. In the 8 years they've been together, she never seen him so frightened and terrified. He looked as if he seen a ghost. She screamed. Before she could run away, Flame leaped upstairs towards her smacking her face with his gun.

"Bitch shut the fuck!", Flame snapped overpowering her then subduing her to the ground. For a split moment, Poncho made a desperate move. He turned on Yatta shoving his arm upwards wrestling for his gun.

Wrestling for his life, for a few seconds there Poncho was getting the best of Yatta overpowering him. But Yatta's youthful abilities worked in his favor, as he somehow and someway slips from Poncho's death grip then slamming his gun so hard to Poncho's face blood sprayed and splattered onto the walls and everything in its way.

"MOTHERFUCKA!!", Yatta said popping him against his face for the second time.

"I should have headshot your bitch ass!", Yatta said hitting him again for the 3rd time and for the sake of Poncho's face hopefully the last.

"Get your bitch ass up nigga!", Yatta hollered angrily still mad at the fact that the nigga had the audacity to try and overpower him. Bleeding profusely from the face confused and delirious, Poncho staggered holding his arms out trying to hold on to the stair railing, the wall or something anything to keep his balance.

"Bring yo ass Bitch!", Flame pulled poncho's girl by her hair. This could be the last minutes of both Poncho and his girl's lives. Thank God that their 13 year old daughter was at a sleep over. It would have been sad for her to lose her young life over such evil, hate, greed, and senseless violence. Knocked out and delirious, Poncho was still standing. His girl was shaking, whimpering, crying, and begging for her life. They both stood in front of their living room couch, before Flame and Yatta pushed them onto it.

"Bitch where the shit at?"

"It's all in the room and the weed is downstairs!", She cried shaking and shivering.

"How much is in there?", Flame asked.

"Forty thousand dollars?", She said quickly as she wept.

"I'm a go check", Yatta told Flame.

"Alright!", Flame replied mean mugging Poncho's girl. Seeing this man in a ski mask with a gun pacing back and forth scared the shit out of Poncho's girl.

"Where's the E pills and Weed?"

"It's all in the room and basement."

"I was living on 75th and Halsted", Poncho slurred talking out the side of his head blacking in and out.

"What the fuck this nigga talking about?", Flame laughed.

"You hit that nigga hard as hell. Come watch this nigga."

"Come on bitch show me where this shit is at?", Flame said snatching on her arm causing her to scream.

"Damn you gotta fat ass!", Flame laughed deviously following Poncho's girl from behind.

"I should get some of that pussy.", He laughed. She was thinking the worst. She's about to get raped and killed. Bleeding from the face struggling to sit up going in and out consciousness, Poncho looked at Yatta and pleaded.

"Come on man. Why are y'all doing this?"

"SHUT THE FUCK UP NIGGA! How much money you got?"

"I don't know man. Where's my daughter? Where's my girl? Y'awl kill them.", Poncho cried. Yatta cocked backed the hammer on his gun.

"And your next nigga, now shut the fuck up!"

Wiping blood from his face, Poncho did what he was told. Retrieving a black garbage bag from the basement, Flame pushed Poncho's girl back into the living room and onto the couch.

"I got the loud and E pills nigga! You can smell this shit", Flame said smiling. Yanking them from the couch, Yatta instructed Poncho and his girl to lay on the living room floor.

"Get on the Flo!", Yatta demanded. Poncho and his girl began to cry loud begging for their lives.

"Please Lord help Please don't kill us!", Both Poncho and his girl cried and pleaded on their knees. From the back of their heads, Yatta pushed them to the floor. Facedown mumbling, crying and pleading for their lives, they begged Yatta not to kill them.

"Please man. We didn't do nothing to deserve this. We didn't do nothing to y'all!", Poncho cried and pleaded as his girl cried for her life weeping loudly. Aiming and swinging his gun at Poncho and his girl's head, Yatta panicked and was ready to shut them up permanently;

"Go see if you can find some more shit.", Yatta panicked. Expecting the unexpected, Poncho and his girl panicked louder then before. Shocked, nervous, and afraid, Flame stood noticing that Yatta was panicking and itching to pull the trigger, hoping he doesn't kill them. Yatta covered his ears with his hands.

"SHUT THE FUCK UP!", He hollered.

"A bro man don't kill them I'm a be right back!", Flame said as he Calmly moved Yatta's hand away from where he was standing over Poncho and his girl faced down crying.

"Jackpot!", Flame hollered, after a few minutes of searching for the weed.

He found the 35 pounds of the reggie weed, and some more e pills.

"This shit is heavy.", he said stuffing the gym bag with the goods as he ran back upstairs into the living room.

"Got it, Let's go!"

"Wait we gotta Kill them.", Yatta said causing both Poncho and his girl to scream, beg and plead for their lives.

"No please no. Sorry God for all the wrong I did.", Poncho cried.

Ready to bust, Yatta stood over Poncho aiming his gun at the back of his head.

"Fam!", Flame snapped. "We don't gotta kill them. We got what we came for let's go!"

"I ain't going to jail or taking any chances they gotta die!"

"No nigga Let's go nigga!", Flame hollered.

Biting his lip Inhaling deeply with his finger on the trigger, Yatta aimed his gun at Poncho's head, shaking his head, Yatta looked at Flame.

"I ain't taking no chances Fam!", Yatta said seriously Flame grabbed both of the garbage bags.

"Fam your tweaking, we got what we came to get man. We didn't come here to kill nobody. I'm out!", Flame said before he ran out of the house.

"Fuck it!", Yatta hollered biting his bottom lip ready to squeeze.

"Don't move if either one of y'all look up. I'm killing both of y'awl you hear me motherfucka!"

"Ok, Ok ok!", Poncho and his girl replied together. Yatta ran out the side door until he caught up with Flame, who was already standing outside of the car with the gym and garbage bags full of goodies. Yatta unlocked the doors and trunk. Flame threw the bags into the trunk before he indiscreetly hopped into the passenger seat while Yatta hopped in the drivers seat. They pulled off their ski masks then sped away.

"Hope you didn't kill em man.", Flame said shaking his head looking at Yatta. Remaining silent, Yatta drove focusing on getting the fuck out of there as far away from Poncho's house as possible as he bent corners slightly speeding. All he wanted to do was make it to the I-57 expressway as quick as possible. Unable to make the green light and caught by the yellow, Yatta had to make a complete stop forcing their bodies upward towards the dashboard. The impact was so sudden Flame smacked the dashboard with his hands to avoid hurting himself.

"Damn nigga you gonna get us caught", Flame snapped.

"I hope you didn't kill them nigga you act like you can't hear motherfucka!"

"Why you tripping nigga? We good!", Yatta snapped back.

"Cuz nigga! I ain't trying to do life in prison, so did you kill them?"

The light turned red. Heading towards the expressway switching lanes, Yatta drives off towards the expressway. Frowning, Yatta turned to Flame.

"You's a pussy ass nigga! We rich as hell and you're up here worrying like a little bitch! If I killed them motherfuckers or not", Yatta snapped.

"Let me call Meechie and let him know we're on our way.", Yatta said merging onto the I-57 expressway.

"Damn nigga! Why the fuck you kill them.", Flame panicked.

Checking both his pants pockets and hood pockets, Yatta looked at Flame.

"You got my phone?", Yatta asked.

"Nawl nigga!"

Speeding down I-57 pannicking and swerving, for a few seconds Yatta took his eyes off the road patting the backseats looking for his cellphone. "Keep your eyes on the road.

"Check the floor and the backseats!", Yatta said hysterically. Bending over the passenger's front seat, Flame searched the floors feeling on the backseats then checking the glove department.

"I don't see our phone man!", Flame snapped.

Yatta checked his pockets again for the 3rd time hoping that his phone would magically appear.

"FUCK!", He hollered.

"I should've went with my first mind and killed them bitches, listening to your ass. I think my shit fell out my pocket when he tried to fight me. FUCK!", Yatta cursed flying past cars down i-57 towards 94w. Flame was relieved; yet nervous, relieved that Yatta didn't kill them but nervous because Yatta had lost his phone at Poncho's house.

Meanwhile, back at Poncho's house, he and his girl were too afraid to move. The house was silent. Bleeding from his face, Poncho turned to his girl.

"Baby I think there gone!", He whispered.

Bursting into more tears and weeping uncontrollably, she cried. Poncho put his arm around her, before he sat up. Walking slowly to his bedroom. He grabbed a dry towel out of the closet and retrieved a handgun tucked under some shirts in the corner of his closet. With one hand, he held his 45 glock gun feeling the rough part of the handle and with the other hand he pressed the white dry towel against his busted and bleeding face walking back into the living room, where his girl was still sobbing and crying still face down, Poncho knelt down beside her gently touching her arm.

"Come on baby get up, it's over their gone.", Poncho said sympathetically. Hating himself for the danger he put himself and his woman in. Crying, shivering, and shaking, unable to keep her balance, she stood up staggering falling into Poncho's arms. Together, they sat down on the living room's couch.

"It's ok baby! We're safe now!", Poncho said hugging her.

"I'm so sorry baby."

"Who was that Poncho?", Belinda asked softly relieved and in disbelief she survived and was able to ask that question, because she just knew that she was going to die.

"I don't know Baby!", Poncho replied.

"Stay right here!"

"Where you going?", Belinda asked frantically afraid to be alone.

"Just to the front baby to check things out!, Be right back" Walking through the upper level of his house, Poncho checked the hallways and bedrooms noticing that they took his safe, money, jewelry, weed and E pills. Angry and pacing back and forth, he stormed out of his bedroom.

"Goddammit!!", He shouted.

"What baby?",

"They got everything!", He said turning on every light in the house walking down the hallway stairs that lead to the garage, on the stairs he noticed a cell then and picked it then put it in his back pocket. Now outside of his house, he checked the driveway and both sides of the house gripping his gun hoping he see one of them motherfucka's now. Once back in the house, Poncho locked all the doors. He pulled out the smart phone he found in the basement then sat next to Belinda.

"What's that?", She asked. Poncho carefully looked at the picture of the young man wearing a Miami Heat baseball cap.

"I know this mothafucka!", Poncho said looking closely at the smartphone scrolling through dozens of pictures. After seeing the same guy in different photos of what seems to be with his friends, siblings, and relatives; Poncho made the assumption that the guy in the photos was the owner of the phone.

"I know this motherfucka!", Poncho repeated to himself thinking and trying his best to figure out where the fuck he seen ol boy in the picture at before? He scrolled through the call history and saw the name Meechie.

"I be damned! That's where I seen this motherfucka he was with Meechie. That bitch made nigga", Poncho snapped.

"What baby? Meechie is behind this."

"Hell Yeah Bae!", Poncho replied.

To confirm his suspicion Poncho called Meechie from Yatta's phone.

"What up Bro! Y'all good?", Meechie answered. Poncho stayed silent shaking his head fighting the temptation to tell this motherfucker how he really feels. He wanted to say motherfucker your dead bitch ass nigga so bad his dick hurted. But he didn't let his emotions get the best of him.

"Hello! Hello!", Meechie repeated looking puzzled.

"Hello! Hello! Yatta?", Meechie said looking at his phone then hung up. Poncho looked at his girl.

"That was him Babe."

"WHAT?", Belinda couldn't believe it. She liked Meechie. She thought he was cool. Meechie earned her respect after Poncho got locked up for 6 months, and he looked out for her and her daughter. He helped with money and even threw their daughter a birthday party.

"Not Meechie, out of all people. Aww! Baby Meechie—say it ain't so.", Belinda complained.

"He would send somebody to come rob and kill us, damn baby. It's some evil ass people in this fucked up world. What if Cherish was here?", Belinda said in disbelief thinking of their 13 year old daughter.

Later that night, Yatta and Flame went back to Meechie's girlfriend's house in Englewood. Yatta was relieved when he saw Meechie's Mercedes Benz in front of the house. He parked behind it.

"Come on", Yatta said hopping out of the car.

"Who is it?", Meechie answered after Yatta knocked on the door.

"It's Yatta and Flame."

"Why you call my and didn't say shit.", Meechie said after opening the door then letting them in.

"I called you back like 5 times and it just kept ringing."

"Maannn! Meechie I think I lost my cell phone at ole boys house.", Yatta said shaking his head as he and Yatta sat on the couch. "Motherfucka tried to fight me and that's when I think my cellphone fell out my pocket.

Sitting on the couch head in hands, Meechie looked up shaking his head.

"Why the fuck y'all take my guns if you wasn't going to use them—STUPID MOTHERFUCKA'S", Meechie hollered.

"You mean to tell me y'all didn't kill that motherfucka and his bitch."

"It was Flame scary ass. He was scared.", Yatta snapped shifting the blame on flame.

"Give me my motherfucking gun you dumb motherfuckas. That motherfucking Poncho called me from your phone nigga.", Meechie said snatching his gun from Yatta's hand. "Where the shit at?", Meechie snapped.

"It's in the trunk."

"Go get it!", Meechie shouted as he stood up pacing back and forth in his living room. Yatta ran out and came back in carrying 2 large black duffel bags.

"Here it is!", Yatta said following Meechie and Flame to the bedroom. He emptied the bags onto the bed. They counted $46,000 in cash $15,000 in jewelry, 285 Epills, 18 pounds of Regular weed, and 3 pounds of Loud.

Instead of taking $10,000 he had intended to take, he took $25,000, all the jewelry, and a pound. Meechie was mad as fuck, their lucky he didn't take it all from them and kill they ass. Yatta gathered up the rest of the goods for him and Flame.

"Y'all fucked up!", Meechie shook his head hot as hell flames.

"Get y'awl shit and get the fuck out my house.", Meechie said slamming the doors behind Flame and Yatta.

Chapter 6

6 A.M: The alarm Clock on the end coffee table besides D.J. Lightbulb's bed blasted loud as hell. He raised his arm slamming his hand down on the alarm clock shutting it off.

"15 more minutes", he whispered to himself closing hi seyes. 10 minutes later he sat up and begin to mentally prepare to carpe diem (seize the day) In a few hours, he was going to have brunch with some very important investors to discuss his next major power move in the making. Then after brunch, he has an on-air interview at WGCI radio station with D.J. Magic Mike and Peaches the midday diva. Then tommorrow morning, he has a 2 hour conference call with Ciara and Chris Brown's managers. After that next Saturday afternoon in downtown Chicago, he will be DJing at the rally for peace and stop the violence juke show with special guests stars Vivica A. Fox, Morris Chestnut, Minister Louis Farakhan, and the Fruit of Islam in attendance. For a local D.J., his schedule was busier than Jay Z's. Lightbulb slipped on his house shoes and went into the kitchen.

Rubbing his eyes, he looked at his fiancé Erica at the dining room table eating breakfast. "Hey Bae!", He said sitting next to her. Lightbulb was very blessed to have Erica in his life, she was 29 years old, successful, and beautiful. Four years his senior, they come across as an odd couple. Lightbulb was a hustla raised in the hood. Fitted baseball caps to the back, Rocawear Jeans, and a stylish sneaker game was his style. In addition, he DJ'd for a living and occasionally smoked weed and hang out with gang members and drug dealers. In contrast, Erica was a clinical therapist. She graduated with a bachelors degree from Southern Illinois, and she was raised in the suburbs of Country Club Hills. Most of her friends were married with extraordinary professional careers. Erica did everything with class, even the way she eats breakfast was done with class. With her fork and butter knife, she elegantly cut a bite size piece of the cheese egg omelet off her plate. It looks like she was doing a commercial for the International House of Pancakes, the way she savored her full luscious lips and sparkling white teeth into the bite size cheese omelet, making it look delicious. Erica was definitely the poster child for a beautiful black woman.

Literally, her skin was dark and smooth like Gabrielle Union. Her long perfectly gorgeous mane brought out her super model features. Like every other day, Erica was dressed for success and ready for work. Beautiful from head to toe instead of her clothes making her look good she made the beige business blouse, skirt, and high heals look good. Eyes bulging at Erica's delicious food on her plate, D.J. Lightbulb smiled.

"Oh snap! Baby—you made French toast, sausage, grits and cheese eggs.", D.J. Lightbulb said excitedly grinning from ear to ear throwing his hands in the air.

"Go Erica go go Go Erica go go, my baby makes the bomb breakfast go go my baby makes the bomb breakfast go go.", D.J. Lightbulb danced shaking in his seat reaching for the carton of orange juice next to the box of Capn crunch cereal box.

"And damn you got the pineapple orange juice joints too—that's why I love your sexy ass!", Lightbulb said grinning cheek to cheek.

Erica sat silently reading the newspaper finishing up the last of her dishes. Smiling, Lightbulb looked baffled.

"So where's my plate Bae?", he asked with a goofy grin on his face. Erica stood up and then put her dishes into the dishwasher. Grabbed her laptops and keys then headed towards the door.

"See you later Babe, I love you."

"Wait...wait hol up hol up hol up Bae?", Lightbulb said.

"Where's my breakfast?"

"It's right there", Erica said pointing at the Capn Crunch cereal box. The corners of Erica's mouth tilted upwards slightly as though she was straining to conceal laughter.

"I gotta go Bae, see you later!"

D.J. Lightbulb looked bewildered and wide eyes, He kept looking around and his eyes kept darting back and forth.

"Erica", D.J. Lightbulb whined. It took everything in Erica's power to refrain from laughing out loud. She cracked a huge smile when she turned her head looking away pointing towards the box of cereal.

"It's right there Bae!", She giggled. Looking as serious as a heart attack, D.J. Lightbulb frowned.

"Erica!", He whined again. "You didn't make me no plate?"

"I told you it's right there.", Erica said laughing softly to herself.

"I ain't eating no damn Capn Crunch cereal and you just had a bomb ass breakfast.", D.J.Lighbulb snapped. "You ain't right GIRL!" Erica was helpless, she couldn't hold it in for another second. She suddenly burst out laughing. You could hear her joyful laughter from a mile away. She laughed so hard the pain in her abdomen made her unable to breathe. D.J. Lightbulb's face twisted into a scowl. He was puzzled and surely didn't see any that damn funny.

"What's funny Erica?", D.J. Lightbulb said seriously. "I'm the hottest thing in Chicago right now. You're a very lucky woman. You're suppose to be my girlfriend. The love of my life and future wife and you didn't even make me no breakfast.", Lightbulb shook his head. "Did you even think about me?"

Looking at Lightbulb's face, she laughed again.

"Oh baby, I needed that laugh.", Erica said grabbing Lightbulb's cheeks.

"Awww baby you're so cute when you're angry. With your gullible self," Erica laughed. "Look in the microwave you gotta great big ole plate of French toast, cheese eggs, sausages and it some cut strawberries in the refrigerator." Erica said before leaving their condo.

Lighbulb didn't know what to do? He was waiting for Ashton Kutcher to burst into his house telling him he just got punk'd. Lightbulb turned his head when Erica tried to kiss him.

"Aww my snookums is mad, I always get you.", Erica laughed.

"Enjoy your breakfast I gotta go, love you.", Erica said leaving out.

"You play too much!", Lightbulb said shaking his head retrieving the plate from the microwave then eating it.

After Lightbulb ate his breakfast, showered, and dressed. He was ready to go handle his business. Dressed for success in his own style. He decided to look like a million bucks, since he was going down to WGCI today with the investors. He was dressed to impress. He borrowed his dress style for the day from Dwayne Wade and Kanye West. He was sporting a light blue suit jacket over a white V neck t-shirt and a pair of Dsquared 2 torn denim jeans priced at $295. On his feet was a pair of White Yves Saint Laurent Rolling leather sneakers, topping it off with a pair of Cardier sunglasses. He even smelled like a million bucks sporting the Gucci Pour Homme Cologne Erica bought him for his birthday.

Lightbulb exited his condo building then unlocked the doors to his all black 2007 Nissan Maxima with the keyless remote. Feeling good, he hopped into his ride then drove away to meet with his investors.

At the brunch, Lightbulb didn't eat much, but he talked the entire time, persuading the investors to his vision and gaining their confidence to invest in the show. After contracts were signed, It was official. March 2008 Spring break weekend, the best Juke dance groups in Chicago will be competing for $50,000 and the chance to dance in Ciara and Chris Brown's music video's.

After brunch, the investors got in their vehicles and followed Lightbulb to WGCI radio station located in downtown Chicago. After they parked their cars, they met up with each other in front of the WGCI building.

"What's up Y'awl? Welcome to WGC and don't forget to dot that I", Lightbulb smiled holding the door for his new business partners Todd and Jamie. Shortly after entering the building, they were stopped by the security guard at the security guard desk.

"And who are you?," The security guard asked Lightbulb.

"I'm D.J. Lightbulb, I have an on-air interview with D.J. Magic Mike and Peaches the midday Diva."

"Oh Ok!", The security guard said fully aware that D.J. Lightbulb would be today's guest in the studio.

Lightbulb and his partners took the elevator to the 7th floor. They were greeted by a cute brown skinned receptionist. Lightbulb couldn't take his eyes off of her. She looked familiar, but he couldn't pinpoint where he knew her from.

"Hello,", The receptionist smiled extending her hand to shake his. "You must be D.J. Lightbulb, I love your mixtapes. My lil sister and her fans always be footworking to you're tapes I even get my footwork on!", She laughed.

"Thank You so much! And yes Live and Effect I'm in the building ", Lightbulb said shaking her hand.

"Follow me", She said coming from around the desk.

"Have anyone ever told you you look like Kelly Rowland."

"I hear it all the time.", She smiled as she opened the studio doors. Inside the studio room, Magic Mike and Peaches the midday Diva were seated in front of microphones listening to Kanye West's classic hit "Through the wire." Magic Mike waved his arm signaling for Lightbulb to come in.

"Lightbulb!", Magic Mike stood up. "What's up man?", Magic Mike said shaking his hand and giving him a bro hug.

"What's good Mike? This is Todd and Jamie my business partners.", Lightbulb introduced them.

"Hey how y'all doing?"

"Good!Thanks for asking, we're just hanging out with Lightbulb.", Todd replied.

"Yeah he's alright.", Magic Mike laughed."

"Have a seat bro!" Lightbulb took a seat front of the guest microphone.

"Get comfortable man, we're gon' play a few more songs then get on with the interview cool?"

"Mos Def", Lightbulb replied.

Kanye West song ended.

"Yeah yeah Chicagoland that was Chicago's very own Mr. Kanye West Classic joint "Through the wire!" Till this day I still love that song.", Magic Mike announced.

"Peaches you remember that video?"

"Hell Yeah!", Peaches replied."

"Through the wire! I love that joint with the Chaka Khan sample. That's when Kanye was normal. I don't know what he is now. I don't know what it is? But Kanye looks like he like white girls.", Peaches laughed."

"He done flipped out calling himself Yeezus.", Peaches said with her unique ghetto sounding voice.

"My favorite part of the video is when all the music stopped and D Ray start rapping", Peaches laughed."

"And damn D Ray is fine as hell too, ooh that man's fine", Peaches said seductively in her ghetto tone.

"So Peaches you mean to tell me tha the only reason you watched the video because of Dray?"

"Yes Child! The same reason you men watch those rap video's with them slutty ass women shaking their asses with no clothes on."

D.J. Magic Mike laughed at the audacity of her comment.

"Chicago do y'awl hear this woman. You're a mess Peaches, Hey D ray if you're listening bruh. You gotta stalker her name is Peaches the midday Diva be careful Bruh.", Magic Mike laughed."

"Shut up Magic Mike", Peaches said playfully.

"I ain't no damn stalker, I just said that the brother is fine and all my ladies out there can agree with that. D ray, I just think you're a fine black man baby.", Peaches laughed with her ghetto ass."

"Yeah Yeah Yeah, Like I said D ray, you gotta stalker bruh be careful."

"You're a hater Mike!"

"Well moving on!", Mike laughed. "Chicago we gotta very special guest in the studio today. I've been knowing this man for many years. He's active in the community. He's a passionate brother. He's Chicago's very own. And he's just a plain ole good brother. Today we got the one and only Juke master D.J. Lightbulb. It's always a pleasure to talk to you. What's going on with you bruh."

Lightbulb's cell phone began to ring "bang bang bang skeet skeet skeet ♬♬♬" After Magic Mike introduced him. Lightbulb immediately turned his phone off.

"Magic Mike thanks for having me man. It's always a pleasure and a blessing to come down to WGCI. I grew up listening to WGCI and it never seem to amaze me that I'm up in here talking to my city. Ain't no city better than Chitown."

"I heard that Lightbulb!", Magic Mike co-signed."

"And for those who don't know Lightbulb, which I can't imagine anyone not knowing you. He's got the number one juke cd out. He's in every major event. A few months ago you did a collaboration with Lil Wayne. How was it working with Weezy F. Baby.", Magic Mike laughed.

"Yeah I met Wayne man. Wayne's a very humble dude and I learned a lot from him. He likes juke music. He actually heard about me. We got in the studio. I did a mix with him rapping on it and everything turned out sweet."

"That's What's Up Lightbulb? Doing things with Wayne, next time you holla at Wayne tell em I need some of that Cash money.", Magic Mike laughed."

"Sooo Lightbulb, I understand that this Saturday. You got something going on.

at Grant Park."

"Can I say one thing", Peaches interrupted.

"What Peaches?"

"I just want to say ladies this brother is smelling good and looking good!", Peaches rolled her neck then smacked her lips.

"I just had to get that off my breast.", Peaches smiled. "I mean chest"

"Thanks Peaches your looking fine yourself.", D.J. Lightbulb blushed.

"Don't tell her that Lightbulb.", Magic Mike said to D.J. Lightbulb.

"Your horny or something peaches you ain't getting none.", Magic Mike laughed. "First D ray now my boy Lightbulb, girl you need some or something. You want me to call my boy Flavor Flav."

"Aww HELL NAWL!", Peaches snapped.

"I have no problem getting me some. They don't call me Peaches for nothing.", Peaches said smacking her lips.

"Ok ok Peaches there's kids listening.", Magic Mike said.

"I gotta get back to my boy Lightbulb before you rudely interrupted us with your freaky self."

"I'm having fun just listening to y'awl", Lightbulb laughed.

"Yeah it's never a dull moment here, so Lightbulb tell us about next Saturday."

"Oh yeah man next weekend in downtown Chicago, I'll be Djing at Grant Park. It's a bittersweet event. It's for our kids whose dying from gun violence in Chicago.

So I put together a juke party for the kids who are no longer with us and bringing together their families and young people to dance, eat, have fun, and celebrate the lives lost to this senseless violence going on in Chicago.", Lightbulb explained.

"It's gonna be games, and a juke show. Minister Louis Farakhan and the fruits of Islam will be there. Celebrity guests Morris Chestnut and Vivica A. Fox will be there speaking. So it's going to be a lot of fun."

"Yeah that's right Morris Chestnut and Vivica Fox will be in the studios next Saturday morning."

Peaches pulled out her Calendar and pointed at the day of the Morris Chestnut interview. On the calendar it read: My husband Morris Chestnut will be in the studios live and in person.

"Yes Baby! I got my hair appointment set and I got my new outfit out of the layaway.", Peaches said fanning herself.

"Oooh Yes Child!", Peaches smiled.

Magic Mike gave Peaches a crazy look shaking his head.

"I don't know what to say about you girl", he laughed."

But on a more serious note, I'm proud of you Lightbulb. We need more brothers like you that does the things you do for our city. It's ridiculous how our kids are killing each other. It's just plain ole stupid man and ignorant. It's gotta stop. It really gots to stop. I'm sick and tired of these funerals. Families are hurt forever. It's destroying our city.", Magic Mike explained.

"But it's brothers like you Lightbulb that keeps my faith alive. You stay close to your community. You haven't got all Hollywood on us. You're humble.

You're real. And with the success you had, you could have easily forgot where you came from and moved to Waukegan somewhere, But that's not you. You're right here in the hood in the heart of things.

And I really admire you Bro.", Magic Mike congratulated Lightbulb.

"I appreciate that Mike.

I know how it is to not have nothing and nobody and leaving Chicago was never an option for me especially with what's going on?", Lightbulb replied.

"Well Lightbulb keep up the good work man.

You're always welcome here at WGCI. And to all y'awl whose just tuning in, we got Juke Master D.J. Lightbulb in the studio.

Next Saturday, bring your kids, family and friends to Grant Park downtown Chicago. There's going to be food. A juke contest and special guests Morris Chestnut, Vivica A. Fox, Minister Louis Farakhan, Me, Peaches the Day time Diva. will all be down there supporting my man's D.J. Lightbulb vision.

We're doing this for Chicago. Stop the Violence.

A Lightbulb once again, it's always a pleasure to have you in the studio.", Magic Mike said pressing a light green square button on the studio boards.

"We gotta pay our bills. When we get back from our commercial break, we got new music from Ciara, some old school Jodeci, and New Jay Z.

So stay tuned to WGCI", Magic Mike said taking his head phones off. Then he stood up extending his hand to shake D.J. Lightbulb's hand.

"Lightbulb Call me man."

"Fo sho! Mike I'm a hit you up.",

"Nice meeting y'all!", Magic Mike said to Todd and Jamie then pointing at D.J. Lightbulb.

"If this guy gives y'all any problems call me!", Magic Mike said jokingly. "Come give me a hug!", Peaches said opeining her arms. After Lightbulb hugged Peaches they left the studio.

Chapter 7

"I wanna freak your body...I wanna feel your body...I wanna touch your body...I wanna sex your body.", RKelly song wild like a zoo played in the background as Lemon moaned in exstacy while Meechie banged her out from the back. Glowing in the dark, Lemon's fat ass jiggled... Meechie banged and smacked Lemon's ass like an African on drums, making it shine redder than Rudolph the rednosed reindeer's nose; After 30 minutes of non-stop fucking and sucking in every sexual position known to man, Meechie nutted once to Lemon's 4th orgasm.

Lemon knew her man's body, so when she felt his body jerking like he was being electrocuted and getting weak inside her. She quickly hopped off his dick and took in all 8 inches of Meechie's manhood into her mouth. She sucked her juices passionately off of her man's Johnson. With his head tilted backwards, Meechie looked up into the heavens as Lemon passionately sucked, licked and kissed Meechie's manhood.

"Damn girl suck that dick!", Meechie moaned with an pleasurable smile on his face. After Meechie nutted for a second time, he wrapped his arms around Lemon collapsing down to the bed. Flopping down together, they fell to the bed.

"Damn I love you girl!", Meechie laughed cuddling Lemon up like a teddy bear.

"Whatever nigga you just love this good ass pussy and bomb ass head nigga!", Lemon said seductively.

"True dat true dat!", Meechie laughed.

"And I love you too, you know your my sweet Lemon head!" Cuddling naked together, they listened to the songs Meechie made specifically for times like this.

"Meechie I think we need to talk, Lemon whispered.

"I'm really feeling our relationship is growing and...and...ah. I really love you, I really do. It's something i've been wanting to tell you to for the past few months I missed my period and I think that I'm pregnant.", Lemon said waiting for Meechie's reply, but instead Meechie began to snore softly. He had fell asleep and didn't hear a word Lemon said.

"Meechie!", Lemon said shaking him.

"What Babe?"

"Did you hear what I said?"

"Uh huh!", Meechie said turning his back to Lemon.

"Damn I was gone, I fell asleep that damn fast. look what that pussy did to me.", Meechie laughed."

"Girl you're gonna be the death of me I was slipping."

"You always fall asleep after we fuck!", Lemon snapped.

"Your pockets be full of money to that's how I know that you trust me. Even If I was a ratchet ass hoe and take your money. I'll be dumb as hell because you already give me whatever I want. I hate when you be talking like that like you don't trust me and shit." Lemon loved Meechie.

She was very loyal to him. She never cheated on him, she hated his trust no one way of thinking, but because of his lifestyle. He had to think that way. He always had to be not 2 or 3, but 4 and 5 steps ahead of anyone he dealt with. He didn't even trust his own mama. But if he only knew the loyalty and love Lemon had for him, he would be more comfortable around her and let his guard down.

"I'm sorry sexy, You know I trust you, I just can't believe I fell asleep that fucking fast."

"Whatever? Stop lieing Meechie.", Lemon punched his chest playfully.

"Now since your ass is up. I was trying to tell you that I'm pregnant baby."

"Pregnant?,", Meechie snapped.

"By who?", He said sitting up in a panic. That wasn't the response Lemon was expecting.

"Who you think nigga?", Lemon snapped...

"I don't know!", Meechie shrugged his shoulders.

"I don't know who you been fucking besides me."

"What Meechie?", Lemon said with a confused frown on her face.

"I can't believe you. Now I'm some type of thot shit fucking everybody now you forreal nigga. I can't believe this shit."

"I thought you was on birth control."

"Oh my fucking God, are you really that fucking selfish, heartless, and dumb.". I thought you loved me.", Lemon said disappointed as fuck looking at Meechie.

"Nobody told your ass to get pregnant.", Meechie said as Lemon sat up. Lemon couldn't believe what she was hearing from Meechie. She knew that he was going to react from the news but not in this fashion. After sitting quietly for a few minutes, Lemon busted out.

"You dumb as fuck, this is your fucking baby I'm having. How you gon say this ain't yo baby and I'm out here fucking everybody.", Lemon snapped.

"Bitch who you hollering at?", Meechie said hopping up from Lemon's bed searching then putting on his boxers.

"Huh? Who the fuck you talking to like that?"

"What? Bitch ass nigga! I'm talking to you", Lemon said jumping up into Meechie's face. She was naked.

Then the unthinkable happened. With his open right hand, Meechie smacked the fuck out of Lemon's face knocking her to the floor startling Lemon's baby sister Aniya who was in the living room watching T.V. A second bang from the room sent Aniya running and screaming to Lemon's bedroom door.

"Lem–mon", Aniya screamed. Only thing Aniya could hear was Meechie hollering and screaming from the other side of the door. Swinging and waving her arms, trying to deflect Meechie's punches, Lemon cried.

"Huh Bitch!", Meechie said with one hand holding Lemon down trying to detain her squirming body and using the other bawled up fist to punch her.

"Don't-ever-dis-re-spect-me-Bitch," Meechie said smashing his fist into Lemon's body and face for every syllable said. Screaming at the top of her lungs, Aniya banged on the bedroom's door frantically.

"LEM–MON", Aniya cried.

Fortunately for Lemon, Meechie stopped. Slipping on his pants, Meechie zipped his pants up buckling his belt, pacing the room like a mad man.

"Bitch you ever disrespect me. I'm a kill yo goofy ass!" Naked, bawled up in a fetal position weeping and crying on the floor, Lemon was to afraid to move, just hoping and praying he would just leave.

"You filthy ass bitch!", Meechie said putting on his shoes and shirt. He grabbed his cell phone and keys. Aniya jumped back when he opened the bed room door then stormed out of the apartment.

As soon as the door slammed, Aniya locked it. Returning to Lemon's room, Aniya looked at Lemon weeping and crying on the floor. Grabbing a blanket from off the bed, Aniya covered Lemon. She sat down next to her and hugged her.

"Don't cry Lemon. He's gone.", Aniya cried.

"I love you Lemon." Lemon was too traumatized to even acknowledge what Aniya was saying. Her love and feelings were so wrapped up in Meechie. The man she loved just physically abused her for telling him that she was pregnant with their baby. She didn't know what to think? Aniya cuddled Lemon's head, as Lemon cried in Aniya's lap.

"It's gonna be ok Lemon!", Lil Aniya assured her.

Chapter 8

Lil Bit remembers the times when she adored, idolized, and loved her Auntie Katherine. To Lil Bit, her Auntie Katherine was a beautiful person inside and out. Auntie Katherine's style was crazy, sexy, and cool. She was popular in their hood. She got any and everything she wanted from boys her age to grown men twice her age from around the way. When Lil Bit was little, Katherine would use the money she took from the boys and men to take Lil Bit and her friends to McDonald's play land, shopping malls, and carnivals.

But now things had changed. Times were different. Auntie Katherine's style and popularity hadn't changed much. She was still Ms. Boss Bitch in the hood. She was still gaming niggas for money getting what she wanted. But the only thing had changed now was the way Lil Bit felt about her. She was beginning to hate and resent Auntie Katherine. That feeling of joy, love, and happiness she once felt for Katherine was turning into feelings of pain, hatred, and sadness. Being around Katherine was beginning to make her sick. Lil Bit knew it was wrong to hate her Auntie, but she couldn't understand Katherine and why she was the way she was.

Taking several pulls from the exotic loud weed rolled in a strawberry flavored cigarillo blunt, Auntie Katherine enjoyed the taste. The exotic loud weed was to strong for her lungs. Blowing out smoke, she coughs hysterically.

"This shit some Fyah!," Katherine laughed passing the blunt to Lil Bit.

"Here you can have this blunt. That's that one hitter quitter. Smoking weed wasn't the only secret Lil Bit was keeping from her mother Marose. If it wasn't for Auntie Katherine, Lil Bit would have never started smoking and drinking. It had become a routine. Smoking and drinking was the only option and escape from the emotional pain of dealing with Auntie Katherine.

Exiting the expressway, Auntie Katherine dialed a number on her cellphone. The closer Katherine approached their destination, the more withdrawn and depressed Lil Bit was feeling. No matter how many times Lil Bit hit the blunt to dull her pain this time it intensified her anxiety.

"Hello"

"Hey! I just got off the expressway. When I get to that road close to your house I'm a call you. It's dark as fuck on that road.", Auntie Katherine said.

"All you gotta do is when you get to Kedzie you drive east a few miles. Then turn right on Dunwoody Drive.",

"I know. I know. I know. Just be expecting my call in 10 minutes. You know I don't understand that east and west shit.", Auntie Katherine explained.

"Ok", The white man said on the other end replied. He was not your ordinary white man. He was an important person. When placed in front of him, he decided rather or not you go free or spend the rest of your life in prison. He was the state of Illinois Cook County Judge. He locked up so many black men, it became a game to him. He decided a defendants prison sentence by how much change he had in his pocket. If he had a $1.15 in his pocket and the crime was something serious like a murder or rape, he would sentence that person to a 115 years in prison. He was one of the state of Illinois crooked judges.

Crickets were chirping and the smell of fresh cut grass filled the air as Katherine drove down a long dark road surrounded by huge three hundred thousand dollar homes. Trying to find Judge Sebastian Phillips home on her own, Auntie Katherine flicked on the headlights high beams. She drove until she approached Dunwoody Road.

"I think this is it!", Katherine said to Lil Bit then dialed Judge Phillips phone number.

"Yes Ms. Katherine!", He answered.

"Yeah I think I'm here I turned on Dunwoody."

"Oh Great!", Judge Phillips replied.

"I'll turn on the garage light. You can't miss my home ain't nothing changed I still got that huge RV in the parking lot. Remember it's 319 Chestnut lane.", Judge Phillips peeped out his door and saw Katherine's driving towards his home.

"Is that you Katherine?", He asked.

"Yes it is!"

"Ok I'll leave the door open come right on in."

Two white bright lights illuminated the front yard of Judge Phillip's 5 bedroom home. Auntie Katherine parked next to the Huge RV.

"Come on Lil Bit this is the cracker I've been telling you about. Girl he got money! He's about to give us some flatscreens, laptops, and anything I ask for.", Auntie Katherine said as she hopped out of her car.

Without responding, Lil Bit did what she was told. She followed Katherine to the entrance doors of this strange man's house.

"Hello Katherine!", Judge Phillips greeted them opening his screen door.

"Come on in make yourself at home.", he said letting them in.

Lil Bit's downcast facial expression made her look sad and embarrassed. With her head down, Lil Bit followed Katherine into Judge Phillips home.

"Hi Hun!", Judge Phillips said as Lil Bit walked passed him. She cringed when he spoke.

"I'm so glad you came Katherine.", Judge Phillips said staring at Lil Bits ass as he locked the front door.

He was selling his home. His wife was at his new home. He had a wife, 2 grown children, a 13 year old son, and a 2 year old granddaughter. Serving as a Cook county judge for many years must've aged him, he was only 53 years old, but he looked at least 60 years old.

"Have a seat guys.", Judge Phillips said giving Lil Bit a cold, evil, calculating smile as he passed them heading towards the kitchen.

"I love this fucking house.", Auntie Katherine said as she sat down, but Lil Bit wasn't comfortable, she stayed standing.

"Thanks Katherine. Want any drinks.", Judge Phillips asked.

"Want something to drink Lil Bit?", Katherine asked her.

. "Yeah", Lil Bit whispered shaking her head up and down.

"Yeah we want some."

First comes the drinks. Next comes the bullshit. The thought of it made Lil Bit's eyes water with tears, but she quickly wiped them away.

"Sit down Lil Bit you're acting weird.", Katherine snapped with an attitude.

"Don't mess this up girl. We finna get a lot of shit."

Judge Phillips came back into the living room with a huge bottle of Patron vodka, Ice, and cups.

"So how was the drive here?", Judge Phillips asked pouring vodka into Lil Bit and Auntie Katherine's glasses. One look at Lil Bit's face and anyone could tell that she was a baby. Didn't he know she was only 16 years old or did he even care. He couldn't keep his eyes off of Lil Bit. His weird sinister stare made Lil Bit get up and move away from him onto the other side of the couch besides Katherine. He jumped up from the couch.

"Hey I got what I promised you Katherine.", He said as he walked away. He came back with a brand new Apple Laptop.

"Isn't that that nice", He asked Lil Bit.

Auntie Katherine rolled another blunt.

After about an hour of smoking and drinking, Judge Phillips stood up.

"Hey can I talk to you Katherine?"

"Sure come on…Be right back Lil Bit", Auntie Katherine followed Judge Phillips into the kitchen. He counted out 20 $100 dollar bills.

"$2000", He said handing the bills over to Katherine.

"She's absolutely gorgeous", He said anxiously.

"Calm down weirdo", Auntie Katherine laughed recounting the money to make sure it was all there. His whole demeanor changed, he seemed not to mind Katherine's insult. In fact, he enjoyed it. He was antsy moving like a child begging for Ice cream.

"Ooh I can't wait to eat her pussy", He said with a perverted smile on his face. Shaking her head at his crazy perverted weird ass, Auntie Katherine chuckled.

"Just take yo ass upstairs and she'll be up there in a few minutes.", Katherine laughed.

"And turn that air off. You white motherfuckers love cold ass houses." Like a 10 year old child, Judge Phillips ran upstairs to his room. Auntie Katherine walked back into the living room and sat next to Lil Bit.

"How you doing Neicy?", Katherine asked. Lil Bit's eyes were bleeding with pain, she didn't know how to answer her Auntie's question. Her face showed distress as she closed her eyes, tear drops slowly ran down her face.

"I don't wanna do this Auntie.", Lil Bit cried.

"I don't wanna do this no more."

Scooting closer to Lil Bit, Auntie Katherine wrapped her arms around her. "Don't cry baby. I know. I know. I know. I know.", Katherine hugged her. "That's why I'm giving you that brand new Apple Laptop and that Flatscreen TV babygirl. I'm tired of this to, but you don't want your grandma to die do you?", Auntie Katherine asked.

"No!", Lil Bit cried.

"Here take another shot of this Patron.", Katherine said pouring a half glass full. Lil Bit downed the whole shot.

"Do you think your mom wants to go to work everyday? No! But she does it anyway because she has to take care of you and Savion. People do things they don't want to do all the time, but they gotta survive.", Auntie Katherine said as she stood up.

"Now come on babygirl. I'm a be in the next room.", Katherine said as Lil Bit followed her upstairs to Judge Phillips bedroom.

"Now go in there and just do what he say ok?", Auntie Katherine said sympathetically pretending like she cared. But all she cared about was the money she was getting for prostituting her own neice. With the flatscreen T.V. on and Judge Phillips laying naked in the bed with a robe on, Lil Bit walks into his room.

"Hi my little sexy black honey. You're so beautiful.", Judge Phillips said with his perverted ass. Lil Bit sat on the corner of his bed with her back turned away from him taking off her shoes. She wiped the tears from her eyes when Judge Phillips begin to caress her shoulders and back. Lil bit stripped down barenaked.

> In 48 hours he'll be sitting at the head of his courtroom presiding over the court. And these are the people our Great United States Judicial system elects to be judges. He should not only spend the rest of his life in prison, but also burn in hell.

Chapter 9

One of the three young men in front of Poncho's house rings the door bell.

"Hey Deion!", Poncho's girlfriend answered opening the screen door letting the 3 young men in.

"Hey Auntie!", Deion says giving her a hug.

"You're ok?", He asked.

"Yeah I can't complain. I'm doing a lot better now."

"That's good Auntie" The 2 young guys followed Deion and the woman upstairs into the living room.

"Where's Unc?"

"He's in the back I'll get him.",

"Pon–Cho!", She hollered.

Deion and his boys Chuck and Lil Herb sat down on the living room couches. Poncho walks into the living room.

"What's up Nephew?"

"Nothing much! What's up Unc? How you doing man?", Deion said pointed towards his friends.

"You know my boys Chuck and Lil Herb right?"

"Yeah I remember these lil niggas what's up y'awl y'awl done got big as hell. "What's good y'awl?"

Rubbing his hands together, Poncho leaned over with his elbows on his thighs.

"Well Deion, we gotta a little problem man."

"Yeah Unc! I remember you telling me man. Fill us in. I'm all ears man."

"Yeah like I said nephew, niggas got me man and Meechie set the shit up."

"You talking about Meechie from the town", Deion asked.

"Niggas been waiting for a reason to get his ass."

"Right right! Yeah he sent too nigga's out here one of the nigga's name is Yatta and I don't know who the other motherfucka was?"

Deion and his boys looked at each other.

"Fuck boy Yatta!", Lil Herb said.

"Hell Yeah! It's only one Yatta from the hood. I seen that nigga yesterday.", Deion said shaking his head looking at Lil Herb interperting his facial expression only a killer would understand.

"And I bet the other nigga name was Flame.", Deion said shaking his head.

"Yeah I know Yatta; we was beefing with them nigga's a few years back, but everything got squashed. I can't believe that shit.

They do be on some grimey shit; but they some fags. Hell Yeah! They fuck with Meechie tough. All them nigga's can get it Unc."

Pulling out 5 crispy one hundred dollar bills, Poncho gave Deion a serious look that meant business.

"I want their heads nephew.", Poncho said handing Deion $500.

"Them nigga's dead Unc. I know where they be and everything.", Deion said pocketing the money.

"I got my hitters too; It's a wrap", Deion laughed.

"Be right back!", Poncho said then stood up and walked to his bedroom. The boys were happy and smiling at each other not because they just got hired to Kill Meechie, Yatta and Flame, but they had some money to go trick off and hang out with some thots.

"Yeahh boyy!", Deion said in his best flavor flav voice.

"We finna get it cracking with Keonna and them. I'm a see if Unc can give us some loud," Deion said smiling then handing Lil Herb and Chuckie each a 100 dollar bill. They shoot and kill niggas for free, but now they were getting paid for it. Yatta and Flame was in big trouble. Poncho walks back into the living room holding an AR 15 assault rifle and a 9 millimeter handgun.

"FUCK IT!," Deion laughed with a devilish smile anxious to get his hands on that assault rifle. Poncho handed it to him.

"Be careful, It's loaded," Poncho warned Deion. Chuck and Lil Herb admired the guns. Deion carefully handed the AR 15 rifle back to Poncho. Poncho looked at him.

"You know how to handle this right?"

"What", Deion snapped looking at Lil Herb and Chuckie with a smile only killers would understand.

"Unc. I know you're all in the suburbs and all, but our whole mob is killers. we got bodies out hear forreal! This is what we do? We the reason they call Chicago Chiraq!," Deion said then stood up.

"Don't even trip Unc, Dem niggas is dead. I got lil niggas that'll lay them niggas out but I'm a do this shit myself personally. It's curtains for Yatta and Flame."

Putting the bullets and magazines into a duffle, Poncho unloaded the weapons into the bag. Wrapping the assault rifle in a blanket he handed it and the 9 millimeter to Deion.

"Take care of them Bitch ass nigga's Deion!," Poncho said with a serious look on his face.

"Don't worry Unc! You'll hear about them niggas on the news", Deion said as he, Chuck, and Lil Herb left out the door.

"Be careful nephew. I love you mean."

"I Love you too Unc!", Deion said before they hopped in his car and he drove off.

Chapter 10

Little girls were jumping double dutch, while Flame talked and entertained Sway and Lemon's fine ass cousin Tatiana that all the boys in the neighborhood was trying to fuck. Yatta was sitting on 24's in his new pimped out whip smoking a blunt with Auriel.

The 14 year old boy wearing headphones, sitting on the concrete steps of a duplex home appears to be just hanging out listening to music. But in actuality, he was on security for the block. A few feet away hidden in the bushes next to the teen was a loaded tech 9. It was just another day in their eastside Chicago neighborhood.

The sun was out and the day was nice. Yatta purposely turned the treble down to boost the bass up in the stereo system so the speakers would bang rattling his trunk.

"I told you Aury, I'll come the fuck up baby you thought ya boy was playing I ain't playing out here.", Yatta said bragging about his new pimped out whip; blowing out loud smoke passing the blunt to Auriel looking at her.

"I told you to stick with me. I told you I was gonna give you everything." Yatta said as he reached behind Auriel's seat retrieving a foot locker box.

"Here Baby!" Auriel opened the box. Mouth wide open and speechless, Auriel couldn't believe it.

"Wow!", Auriel smiled.

"Thanks babe, you really do love me."

"I ain't say I love you I just bought you some shoes."

"Shut up Boy!", Auriel snapped punching Yatta in his chest.

"Oww!", Yatta cried playing hurt. As bad as she wanted to ask Yatta where he was getting all this money and weed from, she left it alone. Deep down in her heart she knew it was all bad. Yatta doing something legit and honest was like Bow Wow being a thug, it'll never happen. Back on the sidewalk, Flame was playing around with the girls.

"Why you wearing them ugly ass shades.", Flame said to Tatiana.

"Cuz I hate looking at thirsty ass niggas like you.", Tatiana replied.

"Whatever you can tell you some kin to Lemon with that smart ass mouth.",Flame said.

"Y'all going to that stop the violence juke show at Grant park. Me and Yatta gonna be there footworking."

"Can the girls footwork?", Tatiana asked.

"Yeah! Everybody's gonna be there footworking. Niggas gonna be battling. Don't act like you knew to this. Be true to this.", Flame said.

"Nigga Please! I live and die for this juke shit.", Sway said smacking hands with Tatiana.

"Niggas and Bitches can get it. I thought you knew I was the Queen of the warzone.", Sway said with confidence bouncing her ass on Tatiana as Tatiana smacked her ass. Flame shook his head.

"Where's Lemon? I ain't seen her all day.", Flame asked.

"I don't even know.", Sway replied.

Meanwhile, a few blocks away. Hopping in Deion's car with the guns Poncho had given them, Deion, Lil Herb, and Chuckie was ready to go change some niggas from living to dead. Deion dialed a number on his phone.

"What's good Pussy?", Deion laughed, talking to Myjuan—a neighborhood flunkee, who was actually a smart kid, but he wanted to be down with Deion, Lil Herb, and Chuckie.

"Why I gotta be a Pussy nigga?", MyJuan replied.

"Cuz you is a pussy. Where you at nigga?"

"Whatever Deion? I'm at the Crib."

"Do me a favor—look outside and tell me whose out there."

"Why?"

"Nigga just do it and stop asking so many fucking questions, I just wanna make sure the fuck boys ain't out there. I wanna buy some loud. Now go see motherfucka."

Pushing the curtains to the side, MyJuan looked out the window.

"Some girls jumping double dutch and Lemon's fine ass cousin Tatiana and that big black bitch with the fat ass Sway and I think that's Flame."

"Flame out there.", Deion asked.

"Yeah and I see Yatta's car to. It looks like he's in there. But you really can't tell, but I don't see no police out there."

"Alright Swalee! Good looking.", Deion said ending the call by pressing the red button on his smartphone.

"Flame and Yatta is out there. Drive!", Deion said in a panic switching seats with Lil Herb who was sitting in the back.

"Hol up hol up!", Chuck interrupted.

"You ain't fenna plan it out!"

"What is there to plan out nigga?", Deion said, making gun shot sounds with his mouth.

"Blocka blocka! That's the plan mothafucka."

Get off that pussy shit!", Deion said seated in the back seat with the assault rifle in his lap anxious and eagered to kill.

"Come on let's do this.", Deion said shaking Lil Herb's shoulder.

Back on Lemon's block, yawning, Yatta stretched his arms out reclining in his seat.

"So when we gonna make us official.

I'm starting to fall in love with that fya ass pussy!", Yatta grinned seductively.

"Stop talking nasty!", Auriel giggled, shifting in her seat.

"Oh Bae I forgot to tell you! We got like 50 thousand views on youtube.", Auriel said speaking about the freak dance they recorded on video.

"You got stalkers boy. Those comments are funny as hell.

One bitch said she wish she was me in the video getting freaked on.", Auriel giggled.

"Why you ignoring my question?", Yatta asked changing the subject quickly.

"I want you to have my Baby? I want to move us out the hood and start a family. I love you!", Yatta whispered the last part of the sentence.

"What you say Yatta?", Auriel replied catching what he said, smiling with warm emotions feeling giggling inside heart skipping a beat.

"Nothing.", Yatta snapped, embarrassed about feeling vulnerable and exposing his feelings, going against the G-code he lives by.

Meanwhile, Deion and his murderous crew actually did come up with a plan. A block and a half away in clear view they were sitting in his car watching Flame kicking it with Tatiana and Sway. They sent Lil Herb strapped with the 40 cal down Lemon's block to clarify and show proof that Flame and Yatta were really out there.

Before their clicks start beefing with each other, Flame, Yatta, Deion, Chuck, and Lil Herb were homeboys. In fact, they were all in the 1st, 2nd, 3rd, 4th, 5th, and 6th grade classes together. It wasn't until high school when they went their separate ways and start hanging out with different clicks that temporarily tarnished their friendships. Their clicks had a few fist fights and a few shoot outs, but no one was killed. Since then their click's beefs were squashed. So seeing Lil Herb strolling down their block, wouldn't be any threat to Flame no way. Passing by with a smirk on his face, Lil Herb made eye contact with the 14 year old hitter as he approached Flame, Tatiana, and Sway. The 14 year old killer was on high alert, getting in position ready to grab the banga hidden under the bushes. A few feet away Lil Herb approached Flame.

"Boy don't be walking up on nigga's like that you know better than that!", Flame snapped with his fist up ready to swing on Lil Herb for scaring and creeping up on him.

"You about to killed out here!"

"My bad boy! I'm just trying to get some loud.", Lil Herb explained.

"Who told you I got loud?"

"Maann you know news travels fast in the hood."

"What you trying to get?", Flame asked.

"A 50...Let me get 4 grams for the $50."

Lil Herb handed Flame a 50 dollar bill. Flame walked over to Yatta's car and knocked on Yatta's car window. A cloud of smoke rushed Flame's face when Yatta rolled down the tinted windows. Flame caught a contact from the exotic smell.

"Let me get 4.0." With his fingertips, Yatta pinched a few buds from out of a sandwich bag filled with Loud weed, dropping the buds onto a digital scale until it read 4.0. "Who want it?", Yatta asked, tying up the plastic bag.

"Lil Herb!"

"Lil Herb!", Yatta snapped with a smirk on his face "Lil Herb nigga. Shit ain't sweet with them nigga's once an opp always an opp. What the fuck you on?

"Man get off that shit. It's just Lil Herb", Flame snapped back.

"You a dumb ass nigga!", Yatta said before exchanging the bag of weed for the $50 dollar bill then pressing the up button on the automatic windows. Flame walked back over to Lil Herb.

"Alright my nigga!", Lil Herb said as he stuffed the bag of weed into his pocket walking off bending the corner. Once out of sight. He calls Deion.

"What's good?"

"Yeah. They both out there Bro! I seen both of them."

"Alright!", Deion said with an eerie excitement.

Putting the assault rifle in position ready to flood Lemon's block with bullets. Deion asked Chuck.

"You ready?", He said. Chuckie pulled off circling the block, so that the passenger's side where Deion was sitting was facing where he had a clear and straight shot at Yatta and Flame.

Preparing to shoot up the block, Deion raised the assault rifle up to the window. Inconspicuously, Chuckie rolled by.

Then all of a sudden he pressed his foot on the gas pedal speeding by.

"What you doing nigga?", Deion snapped.

"My little sisters are out there. I just seen them jumping rope.", Chuckie panicked.

"What Nigga?", Deion said shaking his head.

"Oh my fucking God nigga! Go back to the hood."

"Man my baby sisters are out there. We gonna have to do that shit another time." For a few minutes Flame stared the corner, he just saw Chuckie speed off. He didn't know who was in the car or why they sped away? Standing on the staring at Chuckie's car bending a corner, Flame looked puzzled...

"What's wrong Flame?", Tatianna asked him.

"It look like you just seen a ghost." He knew something was wrong, but he couldn't figure it out.

"Nothing!", Flame replied shaking his head staring at the corner, searching for an answer to why he had a fucked up eerie feeling of death.

Chapter 11

It's been 1 week since Meechie whooped Lemon's ass and blacked her eye. For the past week, Lemon's been avoiding her mama, staying at Auriel's mama's house. When her face and heart heals, she would be going back home.

Auriel entered her bedroom carrying a plate full of smoking hot spicy sausage and pepperoni cheese pizza squares and a 2 liter of hawaian punch.

"Girl, I'm starving", Lemon said hopping up from Auriel's bed reaching for a slice of pizza. Too hot to hold, Lemon dropped the slice back onto the plate blowing on her fingertips.

"Damn girl!", Auriel laughed.

"Big Hungry ass! Wait till it cool down."

"Girl I'm hungry as hell!"

"I see!", Auriel laughed.

"You must be having a boy. You getting big ass hell."

"I know right! My titties and ass is getting fat as fuck.", Lemon said pushing up her titties.

"And girl please tell your little thirsty horny ass brother to leave me the fuck alone.

He's been trying to fuck since I've been here.

Nobody want his lil young ass.", Lemon snapped playfully, reaching and trying for a second time to eat the delicious smelling pizza. Seeking her teeth into the meaty, tomatoey, Italian spicy, cheesy pizza, Lemon moaned like she was having an orgasm.

"Girl this pizza is fya as fuck. I can cum off this motherfucka.", Lemon laughed enjoying every taste of the flavorful meaty, dripping cheese pizza.

"Shut up Hoe! You always got fucking on your mind."

"Nawl!", Lemon laughed. "Forreal girl I can cum off this shit. I love Beggars pizza."

"This ain't Beggars Pizza this is Chicago's Dough Company. You a hoe girl. That's why your thot ass is pregnant now!", Auriel jokedly said taking a bite of her pizza."

Oh! I forgot to telll you, you know Sway and that Lil Bitch. I mean Lil Bit is on there way!", Auriel laughed.

"You gonna let that bitch come in your house.", Lemon snapped, remembering the first time she met Lil Bit.

"I ain't tripping, Sway really like her a lot and I ain't gon lie the bitch do got heat."

"That might be them now!", Auriel said after hearing the door bell ring.

"Answer the door!", Auriel mom hollered from the next bedroom upstairs.

"I am mom.", Auriel said jogging down stairs.

"Hey Sway!", Auriel said opening the door letting Sway and Lil Bit in, then rolling her eyes at Lil Bit.

"Hey Aury!", Sway replied.

"Who is it?", Auriel mom hollered.

"It's Sway mom!", Auriel hollered with an attitude.

"Damn her fat ass is irritating as fuck.", Auriel said underneath her breath, shaking her head.

"Don't be talking about your mama like that.", Sway laughed.

"Hi Ms. Woods!", Sway hollered.

"Hey Sway!", Ms. Woods replied recognizing Sway's voice. Sway and Lil Bit followed Auriel up to her room.

"Is Lemon here?", Sway asked. Auriel opened her bedroom door.

"Yeah I'm here Bitch!", Lemon said sprawled out across Auriel's bed.

"Damn Bitch!," Sway said scrunching her eyes, imagining the pain, Lemon must have went through.

"What happened to you?", Sway asked carefully touching Lemon's face, getting into and examining it...

"I'll tell you later!", Lemon replied frowning her face shying away from Sway. Feeling uncomfortable, Lil bit stood by the bedroom door, looking like an unwelcomed guest.

"You can sit down.", Sway told Lil Bit. She sat down in a chair near Auriel's bedroom window.

"So what's good Bitches?', Sway said flopping down onto Auriel's bed smacking Lemon on her thigh.

"Damn bitch you getting thick as hell. Girl let me tell you about that Bitch right there!", Sway smiled quickly changing the subject pointing towards Lil Bit. "This bitch rght here. My girl Lil Bit! We fenna kill bitches now in any hood. Any warzone, 87th street, West Side, Southside, South Suburbs, Any bitch can get it. We fenna kill hoes. Aint' that right Lil Bit."

"Yeah!", Lil bit said shyly, smiling halfheartedly. Confident and beautiful as ever, Lil Bit held her head up high, but she was as nervous as a black man in court. *I don't know these hoes like that,* Lil Bit thought to herself. And with Auriel and Lemon mugging her like pitbulls, didn't make the situation no better. Noticing the tension in the room, Sway decided to break the ice. Well in Lil Bit's case—break the glacier.

"I asked Lil Bit to be in our group.", Sway said smiling, then patting an empty space on the bed, signaling for Lil Bit to come sit next to them.

"This my girl right here! She's cool as fuck and real. Don't be shy girl."

"I ain't shy!", Lil Bit replied. *I just don't know what the fuck hoes is on?* Lil Bit thought to herself.

"And Lemon, Lil Bit's favorite movie is all of the Fridays. Just like you girl.", Sway said trying her best to soften Lemon's and Auriel's heartstowards Lil Bit. "Yeah I do?", Lil bit giggled.

"I love Day Day and Money Mike. I'm a boy Damon.", Lil Bit laughed, imitating Money Mike versus Damon scene from Friday after next. Auriel smiled a little bit at her comment, but wasn't shit funny to Lemon. It was gonna take a little bit more than common interest to convince Lemon to like Lil Bit's ass.

"And I love the way you dress Lemon, I think you're real pretty and Auriel you look like you can be a model.", Lil Bit said, surprising the girls and even Sway. There was a long awkward silence after Lil Bit complimented Lemon and Auriel. Less than a minute of silence seemed like a lifetime as thousands of thoughts ran through the girls head. Then surprising the fuck out of Sway; Out of nowhere Lemon replied with a forgiving smile. "Thanks!"

But after spending the past week with Lemon, Auriel wasn't surprised at all. She noticed a change in Lemon's attitude since the first day Lemon came knocking at her door standing at her doorstep with a stuffed Gucci bag full of clothes hanging out of it crying, asking Auriel if she could stay over for awhile. Auriel will never forget that day, Lemon looked like she was in a car accident. Her hair was wild and messy. Her eye was swollen and her face was bruised and red. Crying and distressed, Lemon could barely speak. Auriel knew it was serious. She wrapped her arms around Lemon and let her in. It seemed like ever since Meechie whooped Lemon's ass and she found out she was pregnant. Her attitude had changed alot, knocking her off her high horse back down to reality. The next morning, Lemon explained everything to Auriel—that after she and Meechie has just made love, he beat her half to death for telling him that she was pregnant with his child. Lemon went on to tell Auriel how much she loved her like a sister and thought she was so beautiful and apologized to Auriel for all of the times she hurt her feelings and made her feel bad. The girl was already suffering traumatically. She didn't bother to tell Lemon how much she hated her for all of those ridicules, and put downs. Through it all, Auriel loved Lemon like a sister. Although, she had always admired Lemon and she had forgiven her, she couldn't help but think to herself that it took an ass whooping for Lemon to respect and be nice to her. The Bitch should've got her ass whooped long time ago. But Auriel knew that was mean and at the end of the day, Lemon was her sister.

"You're welcome!", Lil Bit smiled exhaling with relief, no longer worried about being in Lemon and Auriel's presence. Something about Lemon's facial expression and demeanor, made Lil Bit believe that she was sincere. Sway went into her purse, retrieving a sandwich bag half way filled with weed.

"Damn! Where you get that from?", Auriel asked.

"Flame—he just gave it to me."

"What?"

"Yep! Roll up!", Sway said handing Auriel the bag of weed and a pack of cherry wine cigarillo's.

Lighting two incense, Auriel placed a white fluffy dry towel under the crack of her door. By the end of the night, Lil Bit grew on Lemon and Auriel. They could see why Sway liked her so much. She was one of them. They knew the same people. They were from the same hood. They loved the same music and movies. They loved to dance. They shared the same struggles. They were just 4 teenage girls from Chicago—Trying to Live. They ordered Chinese food and smoked the whole pack of cigarillos. Laughing and watching Friday after Next, they were higher than giraffe asses. Initially, what was intended for Sway to introduce Lil Bit to the girls had turned into a slumber party. They discovered that Lil Bit was their missing link. Lil Bit was not only the newest member of the L.O.A girls, but their bond was the beginning of new friendships. From the start, they kept it 100 with each other. Lowkey, they knew Lil Bit was the best dancer of the group. But they could live with that, because they complimented each other well. They practiced dance moves, talked, laughed, and joked until Auriel, Sway, and Lemon fell asleep. But Lil bit was still awake. Ever since her Auntie Katherine made her sleep with the first perverted trick two years ago, every night Lil Bit had been having trouble falling asleep. Watching her beautiful new friends sleep and thinking about all the fun they just had, made Lil Bit smile. But now the fun was over. Like a light switch, Lil bit was turned back off into the darkness full of sadness, shame, and guilt. When Lemon was telling her story behind her swollen and bruised face, Lil Bit wanted to share her secret to. Deep down in her heart, she knew that her secret was safe with them. But she was to ashame to tell anybody. The secret was killing her. She had to tell somebody. It hadn't been a single night since 2 years ago that she didn't want to kill herself. With a blank emotionless expression on her face, she watched her friends sleep, until like every other night in her troubling life, she cried herself to sleep.

Chapter 12

"Hey Hey! Chi-Ca-Go", Magic Mike said into a microphone headset standing beside a stage in front of a crowd at the Stop the Violence Juke show at Millineum Park with his co-host Peaches the Midday Diva. Magic Mike turned to look at Peaches.

"You're having fun here Peaches.", He asked her.

"Am I having fun?", Peaches said rolling her neck.

"Do an elephant gotta big ass? Hell Yeah I'm having fun.

I'm having the time of my life. I just met my future husband Morris Chestnut. So ladies he's taken he's off the market thank you! And thank you!", Peaches said smacking her lips.

"And yes my new name is Peaches Chestnut and don't forget it!", Peaches snapped her fingers.

"You a mess!", Magic Mike laughed shaking his head.

"Y'all heard that. It's going down out here at Grant Park—Peaches is having fun, I'm having fun. Are y'all having fun?", Magic Mike asked the crowd.

The crowd went crazy cheering.

"Y'all heard that! So stop whatever you're doing and get your butt down here. Bring your family. Bring your kids. Bring your baby mama.

Bring your baby daddy.

I don't care who you bring just get your butt down here.

It's so many grills going out here. I feel like I'm at family reunion.

The ladies are looking good. Y'awl here the background,

That's Chicago's very own Bump J up there rapping.

We got Vivica Fox out here. Peaches Husband Morris Chestnut;

We just doing the damn thang. Here comes the man that made this all possible.", Magic Mike said looking at D.J. Lightbulb approach him.

"What's up D.J. Lightbulb?", Magic Mike said slapping his hand then handing Lightbulb the microphone.

"You're live on the radio."

"Oh yeah! That's what's up?", D.J. Lightbulb smiled a debonair and charming grin immediately getting into character.

"Yeah Yeah! What up Chicago? It's ya boy D.J. Lightbulb and we out here at Grant Park. The weather is beautiful.

I couldn't ask for a better day for this event. You know this event is for a good cause. I love my city and it hurts me that my people are out here killing each other. So every chance I get I do something big for my city to help bring us together man. I just met Vivica A. Fox, Morris Chestnut, and Minister Louis Farakhan and they didn't ask for no money. This event is not for profit. They came out from their busy schedule to come be with us Chicago.

This is for the people we lost out here in these streets and it really needs to stop. So come on out. If you lost a love one, a brother, a sister, a friend or a person you know. Come on out for them. We're celebrating their lives man. It's thick out here. The young men out here is about to turn up juking.", D.J. Lightbulb said looking up on stage.

"A yo my boy Bump J is about to get off stage. I gotta go but I love y'all Chicago man come on out to show your support.", D.J. Lightbulb said leaving for the stage. Microphone in hand, D.J. Lighbulb ran on stage looking like a NBA player—wearing Jordan number 23 jersey, shorts, shoes, and bulls hat to the back with a long diamond platinum chain hanging around his neck.

"How y'all feeling out there?", D.J. Lightbulb said sniffing the air.

"Damn! can somebody make me a plate. The barbeque is smelling good out there—I want y'all to give it up for my boy bump J.", D.J. Lightbulb said causing the crowd to cheer.

"I have a very beautiful special lady that's coming to talk to y'all today. She lost her 16 year old daughter Shakira Thompson and she doesn't want another mother or family to go through what she's been going through. So lend your ear and heart and listen to her. I want y'all to give a warm welcome for a very special inspiring lady Ms. Diane Thompson!"

Wearing a purple T-shirt with her daughter's picture on it, Diane Thompson walks center stage.

"Thank you Lightbulb!", Diane whispers along with a gentle smile. After hugging her, Lightbulb handed Ms. Thompson the microphone. Before giving her speech, she looked at all the beautiful black faces in crowd applauding her. For a moment she absorbed all their sympathetic and loving faces. She especially empathize with the other families who were out in the crowd wearing T-shirts with the faces of their fallen love ones on them.

"Thank you so much?", Diane smiled.

"Thank you! Thank you! Thank you!", She said softly into the microphone. For a few moments she paused collecting her thoughts.

"You know I'm wearing purple today because this is my baby's favorite color.", She said smiling.

"I'm usually a shy person and I can hear my baby saying mom stop being so shy", She said with a smile.

"So all of this is for my baby Shakira", Ms. Thompson said looking around and into the crowd at all the young white, black, puerto Rican, and many faces. "Shakira was amazing. She had a huge heart. She loved to laugh. She was quirky. She loved life. She was just a kid!", Ms. Thompson said fighting back tears and voice crackling with grief.

"She loved to dance. She loved to footwork. Oh my God! she loved that juke music and footwork so much, she got on my nerves with that mess. She use to run in the house and say mom—you need to hear this new D.J. Lightbulb mixtape. I use to say D.J. Who?", Diane laughed, before bowing her head down in silence for a moment gathering up the courage and strength to finish on. Overcome with grief, LightBulb came to her aide, but she manages to finish.

"No parent should have to go through this.", Ms. Thompson cried exhaustingly jumping from emotion to emotion trying to keep herself together.

"The passing of my daughter has touched the whole city of Chicago.

The support I've been getting has been amazing.", She cried nearly fainting but staying strong.

"I'm not worried about my baby's soul. She's in a better place but please please stop killing each other.", Ms Thompson said softly crying then leaving the stage unable to finish, leaving the crowd in tears. Her plead to the city of Chicago touched everyone. Lightbulb shook his head after hugging Ms. Thompson then taking the mic.

"This really need to stop!", Lightbulb said with frustration.

"Please Chicago, I'm begging you. Please STOP THE KILLINGS!", D.J. Lightbulb said leaving the stage on that note as the music technician played.

"Smile" by Kirk Franklin for the intermission.

Vivica A. Fox, Morris Chestnut, and Minister Louis Farakhan supported Ms. Thompson and the families of victims. Each celebrity and public figure had their own turn speaking on the importance of stopping the violence in

Chicago and living for the future. After their speeches, twenty of Chicago's best young men juke dancers battled each other on stage including Flame and Yatta. Although juking wasn't their thing, Meechie and his gang were there on stage having fun supporting Flame and Yatta. While Flame and Yatta were enjoying themselves dancing and showing off their footwork skills and talents on stage; Lurking in the crowd without taking their eyes off of them, Poncho, his nephew Deion, Chuckie, and Lil Herb looked at them like madmen. Although, the purpose of the event was peace and stopping the violence, nothing close to peaceful was on the minds of Poncho, Like wild animals on a sneak attack, they just stared at Meechie, Flame, and Yatta amongst the crowd of hundreds of people.

Chapter 13

For the entire day, Lil bit and Auriel were innocent onlookers watching the tension between Sway and Lemon get thicker than Amber Rose's ass and thighs. From the time Sway picked up Lil Bit, Auriel, and Lemon at 10 a.m. in her auntie's car. To the shopping mall where they went shopping for Tomorrow's talent show—leading up until now, where Sway and Lil Bit were sitting and waiting at the beauty shop on 83rd street for Lemon and Auriel to finish getting their hair done—things were getting messy between Sway and Lemon. For the whole day they said very few words to each other, but their attitudes, eyes rolling, and facial expressions spoke volumes. Lil Bit didn't know what to expect next, she was sitting there looking confused yet fine as fuck in her new gorgeous flowing beachy waves reverse ombre hair style with her hair fading from light to black. And Sway was sitting down mean mugging everybody in the beauty shop yet looking sexy as hell in her new poker-straight smooth blonde lace front hair style. Bitch you need to hurry up! It's almost 1 o'clock in the morning.", Sway snapped at Lemon impatiently rocking her right leg crossed over her left one. Sway was pissed, she couldn't believe Lemon went back to Meechie after he whooped her ass. In her mind, Lemon was the dumbest bitch in the world. Sway could care less about the fact that Lemon took them shopping and got their hair and nails done for tommorow's talent show with the $2500 Meechie gave her. No large amount of money in the world would make Sway ever go back to a nigga that blacked her eye and bruised her face. That motherfucka will be dead as a fuck as far as Sway was concerned. She wish a nigga would. If she ever showed up in front of her 5 brothers with a black eye from her boyfriend—that nigga will be on the first 48.

"You're an ungrateful Bitch! You know that Sway.", Lemon said from the stylist chair she was sitting in.

"Why you worried about me and my man? He's sorry for what he did.

He gave me $2500 and I took y'all bitches shopping and this is the thanks I get Yo! ungrateful ass with your funky ass attitude fuck you mean!",

"What Bitch?", Sway snapped. If it wasn't for the stylist finishing Sway hair, Sway would've jumped out her seat and popped Lemon in her face.

"FUCK YOU MEAN!", Sway snapped rolling her eyes.

"You a dumb hoe, getting back with that nigga! I tell you what bitch.

Just don't come back crying to us when that nigga whoop yo ass again.

That's all I gotta say." The beauty shop got quiet as a library. The beauticians, Auriel, and Lil Bit was speechless. They felt bad for Lemon, but they kinda felt where Sway was coming from. Low key Lemon was crying in the stylist chair, but she wiped her face. Everybody saw it accept Sway. Even if Sway saw Lemon crying, she wouldn't give a fuck anyway about the dumb bitch's feelings. It was time to pay the stylist. Lemon pulled some 50's and 20's out of her purse and paid the beauticians. Looking like a million bucks, rocking that Rhianna colorful short, straight red hair and bangs to the side, with her head down, Lemon walked over to Sway's stylist and paid her too, handing the stylist her a $100 bill and some 20's.

"Thanks girl!", The stylist said to Lemon.

"You're welcome.", Lemon replied with her head down. Lemon was hurt. She knew Sway was right. Noticing Lemon was hurt as the girls left the beauty salon, Auriel wrapped her arm around Lemon. During the trip home no one spoke to each other as Sway dropped them all off. They were mature enough to know that what ever differences they had, they had to get over it. Tommorrow was their big show.

Chapter 14

All of the dance groups were backstage waiting for D.J. Lightbulb. The auditoriom was packed with people ready to watch the show. As the waited for D.J. Lightbulb, all six of the dance groups were sizing each other up, while D.J. Lightbulb explained the rules of the talent show. Staring at the groups sideways, Lemon rolled her eyes.

"Are we the only ones that got our hair done these bitches look popped.", Lemon whispered to Auriel.

"I know right and did you see them niggas them dudes in that one group look gay as hell.", Auriel replied.

"Ugh! You see them hoes dirty ass socks and clothes!", Lemon whispered in Auriel's ear frowning her face.

"These hoes hair ain't done or nothing. I feel like I'm over dressed. This old ghetto ass talent show.", Lemon complained.

"Only hoes that looks half way decent is fee fee and them and they some thots.", Auriel added, before Lightbulb spoke.

"Now!", Lightbulb said with a pen and pad in hand.

"I need to know the names of y'awl dance groups", He said pointing to the largest of the groups with 8 dancers in it and afterwards pointing to the rest of the groups.

"We're Total Domination!", They replied.

"Fearless Squad", The youngest girl of their group answered.

"Ladies of Action", Sway answered.

"76th street Boss Bitches", Fee fee answered...

"Notorious Diamonds!", The girl with the big ass answered.

"Fearless Squad.", another girl answered.

"And y'all back there?", D.J. Lightbulb said pointing towards the back. "We're the footwork Queens and can't nobody mess with us.", The cute little girl in the group said with confidence. D.J. Lightbulb wrote down the names of their groups and took the songs down they wanted played.

"Ok Y'awl know this is gonna be an important talent show.

There's going to be 6 winners that move on to the finals in 2 months.

We got some important people coming out. We got 106 and park producers coming and we also got Ciara and Chris Brown coming.

The winner of that show gets a chance to be in Chris Brown's and Ciara's music videos and also win $50,000.", Lightbulb said causing the members of each group to smile and chatter about the hopes of winning $50,000.

"Ok! Y'awl each got 3 minutes. Do your best out there and there's no losers y'awl are all winners have fun and do your thang! And thank you all for being in the talent show.", D.J. Lightbulb finished heading towards his D.J. booth on stage in front of an auditorium full of teenage kids.

Chapter 15

Right before midnight, the party on 81st street was turnt up. Loud music was banging from the house where there were teenagers were hanging out on the porch. Cars rolled up on the block with teenagers and young adults hopping out of them playing around with each other. Loud smoke and excitement was in the air. Inside, the house was packed with rowdy teenagers and young adults in their 20's dancing, popping mollies, and smoking.

Among the partygoers inside, Flame and Yatta were footworking with Auriel and Lil Bit. It took a lot of convincing on Auriel's and Flame's behalf to get Lil Bit to come to the party. But they ultimately succeeded, for the first time in a long time Lil Bit was enjoying herself dancing and footworking at the party. Blowing back loud with the girls and friends at the party and gripping the bottle necks of 1800 vodka and hennesy, Flame and Yatta were high and drunk as hell stunting on niggas and bitches. It was coming up on 2 months since Flame and Yatta robbed Poncho and his girl. They were beginning to relax letting their guards down. If they were found out by the police or any of Poncho's people, something would've had happened by now. But no that wasn't the case, they was alright. That's what they thought. But the whole time, their enemies were right under their noses. That eerie feeling of death Flame felt that day on Lemon's block, when he saw that car suddenly stop then swoop away was real. For the whole night and from a distance, they had 6 eyes watching them. Deion, Chuckie, and Lil Herb was at the party too and they didn't come there to dance. In fact, when Yatta and Flame seen Deion, Chuckie, and Lil Herb 20 minutes ago, Flame said what up to them. But with Yatta's fuck all opps attitude, he didn't say shit to neither one of them.

A few hours had passed and the party was winding down. Deion, Chuckie, and Lil Herb were among some of the few people that left early.

It was not because they were going home. But because they were going to Deion's car to wait on Flame and Yatta to handle that business Deion had promised his uncle Poncho months ago. Squinting his eyes from a distance looking carefully, Deion hopped up in his seat when he saw 4 more teenagers leaving the party house.

"That's not them.", Deion said shaking his head.

"Scary ass niggas taking long as fuck to come out.", Deion snapped unlocking the car door—placing the 40 cal gun in his jacket pocket.

"What you bout to do?", Lil Herb asked.

"I don't want these niggas to slip away, So I'm a just wait in the gangway until they come out.", Deion replied before hopping of the car crossing the dark street walking towards the house. He found a low key spot in the gangway beside the party house. After, waiting 20 minutes, Deion finally noticed Flame and Yatta. Yatta, Flame, Auriel, and Lil bit walked out on the porch. They were fucked up and feeling good. Tonight was Flame's lucky night, he had been trying to fuck Lil bit ever since he broke Lemon and her up from fighting that day. His hard work was about to pay off. But what was about to happen next was going to fuck everybody's night up. Creeping closer to the side of the party house, Deion quietly pulled the 40 cal out of his pocket. With their arms around Auriel and Lil Bit, Yatta and Flame clumsily stepped down the porch steps. Adrenaline rushing through his body—gun shaking in his hand, Deion kept a close eye on Yatta and Flame as they stepped onto the sidewalk with Auriel and Lil Bit who were trying their best to help them keep their balance.

"Boy! You're gonna have some fun tonight.", Yatta slurred after peeping out the corner of his eyes at LilBit's booty in the tight jeans she was wearing.

"He ain't getting nothing here!", Lil Bit snapped.

"Where you park at nigga?", Flame said changing the subject—hoping Yatta didn't fuck up his pussy for tonight. Pointing in the direction of where Deion's car was parked where Chuckie and Lil Herb was sitting, they began walking in that direction. Taking a deep breath, Deion ran out from the gangway. A split second after Yatta hollered.

"OH SHIT!" and Auriel screaming. 9 shots rang out. "Pop.pop.pop.pop. pop.pop.pop.pop.pop!" Yatta tried reaching for his gun, but before he could get a good grip on it, he collapsed to the ground. It all happened so fast.Taken by surprise, Flame froze up watching his friend fall to the ground as Auriel and Lil Bit ran back into the house. Snapping out of shock, Flame jumped into action grabbing Yatta's 40 cal out of his hand. Running and gunning Pop.pop.

pop.pop.pop" Flying down the street Flame chased after Deion, Flame caught up to him. Falling like a wide receiver going into the in zone, Deion tried his best to keep his balance, but the 3 bullets that struck him in his back caused him to collapse in the a street an arm reach away from his car. Already in the driver's seat—Lil Herb drove away running over Deion's hand. Flame shot twice at the car, before he stood over Deion body finishing him off with a last shot to Deion's face. Running back to his best friend Yatta, Flame hollered.

"HELP!", But it was too late—Yatta was laying as still as a door knob. He had already died. A block away from each other one on the sidewalk another in the middle of the street, two young black men lay dead. An all too familiar sad scene was taking place as Partygoers were coming outside and Auriel screaming and crying over Yatta with Lil Bit trying to comfort her. Flame couldn't even look at his friend no more—gun in hand, he cried. The coroner, police, and firemen had rolled up. As Flame was being instructed by the police to put his gun down, he cried with his arms in the air. "They killed my Bro! They killed my Bro!", Flame cried tossing his gun to the crowd surrendering to the police he was handcuffed then shoved in the back of the police squad car. Wishing it was all a dream, from the backseat of the squad car Flame cried as the police drove him away to cook county jail.

Chapter 16

Rehearsing the same dance move over and over again, Lemon wasn't getting it. Plus she was tired. Her feet was aching from the extra pounds she had put on from being pregnant.

"Where's Auriel and Lil Bit?", Lemon said out of breath leaning on the wall railing shaking her head.

"Lil Bit's on her way and I've been calling Auriel all day, she ain't picking her phone up. I haven't heard from her in 2 days.", Sway answered.

"Last time I spoke to her was the night she went to that party with Yatta and Flame.

"Lil Bit didn't tell you.", Lemon responded.

"Tell me what"

"Yatta got killed!"

"What?", Sway said. She was shocked.

"Yeah! 2 days ago he the one who got shot at that party and Flame killed the dude that killed Yatta that same night. Now he's in jail for murder."

"Damn! That's fucked up.", Sway replied.

Sway couldn't believe it, Yatta and Flame was her dudes.

"Where's y'all other 2 dancers?", D.J. Lightbulb asked walking back into the dance studio.

"Lil Bit's on her way and we can't get in touch with Auriel."

D.J. Lightbulb was so impressed with the girls at the talent show he took on the role as their mentor and manager. He booked out time at a local dance studio, so the girls could practice. But there was always something with the girls. One or two was always absent or late for practice and when they would be there, they would argue and fight all the time.

"Take a 20 minute break. We gonna wait till Lil Bit get here.", D.J. Lightbulb said leaving the dance studio.

"When you're gonna tell Lightbulb you're pregnant?", Sway asked Lemon.

"I'mma tell him.", Lemon said getting defensive.

Finally after Lil Bit showed up the girls practiced every dance routine there was for the rest of the evening. Auriel never showed. She was still grieving over Yatta's murder. D.J. Lightbulb understood how life in their hood was for the girls.

He was determined to not only make the girls better dancers but make them better people.

Chapter 17

Weeks had passed since the shooting of Yatta and the hood was still healing from it. Thanksgiving was in 2 days and Sway was telling Lemon about the funeral.

"Girl it was so sad.", Sway explained over the phone details of Yatta's funeral to Lemon.

"His mom wouldn't let him go, she just laid on him. It was the saddest funeral I ever been to seeing his little sisters crying. I see why you hate funerals."

"I know girl. I still can't believe he's dead. I miss him so much. He use to always tell me that I'm having a boy and to name him Deeyatta. That boy knows he was a mess.", Lemon smiled remembering the good times with DeeYatta.

"Did you tell you're mama that you're pregnant yet."

"I'm thinking about telling her today."

"You might as well she gonna find out anyway. What you think she's gonna do?", Sway asked.

"I don't know girl. That's what I'm worried about.", Lemon said.

"I gotta go girl, Aniya is in here bothering me. I'm a call you later.",

"Ok Bye Lemon.", Sway said pressing the end button on her smartphone.

Hopping in bed with Lemon, Aniya rubbed her stomach.

"What you doing girl?", Lemon said to Aniya.

"Rubbing my nephew."

"What if you're nephew is a girl?"

"But I don't want a neice. I want a nephew.", Aniya whined.

"I like Antonio. Ain't that a cute name for my nephew."

"Antonio!", Lemon laughed.

"Aniya really! Where you come up with these names, that's an old ass man's name. If it's a boy! I'm a name him Seantrell."

"That's a cute name, but I like Antonio better.", Aniya said laying beside Lemon looking up at her.

"Ugh!", Lemon grunted.

"I'm a let you help me name my baby, but I don't know about Antonio. I'll think about it. Now get out of my bed with your shoes on. I told you about that girl."

"LEMON!", Their mom hollered from the living room.

"Here I come Mom!"

"You're gonna tell mom you're pregnant?", Aniya asked as Lemon sat up.

"No girl! Shut up girl dang!", Lemon snapped getting up out of her bed to go see what her mother wanted with Aniya tagging along from behind as usual.

"Yeah mom!"

"Can you run to the store and get me some cooking grease and jiffy mix. I'm almost done with thanksgiving dinner.", Her mom said handing her money.

"Oh and get some dishwashing liquid and a 2 liter of hawaaian punch to."

"Ok!", Lemon replied. "Oh Mom, I gotta talk to you about something when I get back.

"About What?"

"I'll tell you when I get back mom."

"Mom can I go with Lemon", Aniya asked their mom.

"It's getting late Aniya."

"She's ok mom.", Lemon interrupted.

"It's still light out.", she explained.

"Ok hurry back!"

Holding Aniya's hand, she and Lemon walked down the block of their east side neighborhood.

"If mom gets mad at you for being pregnant Lemon, I just want you to know that I won't be mad at you. I can't wait to see my little Antonio"

"Girl you must like some boy name Antonio I'm not naming him Antonio girl.", Lemon laughed.

"I told you that girl stop bugging me about that name."

"Lemon!", Aniya said doing her baby sister duties by pestering Lemon.

"What Aniya?"

"I wanna dance with y'all in front of Chris Brown. Girl he is so fine!"

"We're not dancing with them yet Aniya. And if we win were gonna be his and win $50,000"

"Fifty thousand dollars!", Aniya replied. "That's bands!"

"Girl where you're learning all that slang"

"106 and park!", Aniya replied causing Lemon to laugh.

Walking towards them was a boy Lemon knew from around the neighborhood.

"You wanna buy a taser?", He asked then pulling it out squeezing the handle of the taser causing it to crack with electricity. Jumping back, Lemon snapped.

"Boy stop playing!", She said guarding Aniya.

"Let me see that!", Lemon said snatching it out of his hand.

"How much you want for it?", She asked. Nervous and looking over his shoulder the young man noticed a half-a-block away, a yellow monte carlo sitting at a stop sign.

"Keep it!", he said before immediately walking away leaving Lemon puzzled and confused.

"Thanks!" she replied holding the taser in her hand.

"Come on Aniya!"

Burning rubber moving at top speed, the yellow Monte Carlo sped to the middle of the street screeching to a halt. Next the unthinkable happened.

"pop.pop.pop.pop.pop.pop.pop.pop.pop.pop.pop"

Shots ring out. Pulling Aniya by her hand, she and Lemon ran fast.

"LEM-ON!", Aniya screamed letting go of Lemon's hand collapsing to the ground.

Burning rubber, the Yellow Monte Carlo sped off. A few yards away, Lemon ran towards Aniya.

"ANIYA!", Lemon shouted panicking from the site of Aniya's blood soaked shirt. Dropping to her knees, Lemon cried.

"Get up Aniya!", Lemon cried.

"HELP! SOMEBODY HELP ME!", Lemon screamed.

"Lemon! I can't breathe", Aniya cried.

"Mommy...Mommy!", Aniya cried breathing heavily gasping for air as tears rolled down her face.

"HELP SOMEBODY HELP! CALL THE AMBULANCE!", Lemon screamed.

"Aniya you're gonna be ok, just keep breathing. PLEASE HELP SOMEBODY HELP PLEASE! THEY SHOT MY BABY SISTER", Lemon cried losing her mind.

"I don't wanna die Lemon!", Aniya said losing consciousness.

Some young men ran up with their cell phones to their ears. One of them got a hold to 911.

"A little girl just got shot out here we're on 72nd and Merrill, hurry up please hurry up it looks like she's dieing.", One of the young men told the 911 dispatcher.

"Aniya!", Lemon said shaking her.

"Oh my God! Aniya! Aniya say something.", Lemon cried.

Chapter 18

In downtown Chicago, the time was approaching the dusk of the day—the period of partial darkness between day and night. Crowds of people were in commute leaving work to go home. Buckingham fountain illuminated with changing colors. Tall buildings and skyscrapers illuminated the dusk skies. Located in the Sears Towers building was the offices of Jamie Sullivan's and Todd Metzger's Investment company located on the 99th floor. In Jamie Sullivan's executive office suite, he looked out of the glass window—overlooking Wacker drive and the Chicago River while Todd sat on an expensive plushed leather couch. Jamie pulled a quarter out of his pocket.

"Let's flip on it!", Jamie said to Todd.

"Heads you break the bad news to D.J. Lightbulb that we will not be funding his event or tails I will tell him."

"Ok!" Jamie flips the coin.

"Tails! Fucking A!", Jamie snapped.

"2 out of 3"

"No that wasn't the deal!", Todd replied with a chuckle.

"Why don't you just fund the stupid event?

We have the money. And I like Lightbulb he's one of the good ones." "No Todd!", Jamie replied pacing the floor of his executive office looking out the huge glass window.

"That nigger event and nigger dancing isn't profitable and they may end up shooting someone after it's over anyway. You know how them niggers are—there like animals."

"Yeah you're right about that!", Todd laughed.

"So get to dialing." Placing the call on speaker phone, Jamie dialed Lightbulb's number.

"Talk to me!", Lightbulb answers his cell phone laying on the couch with his fiance Erica on top of him—they were watching their favorite movie Love and Basketball.

"Hey! How's it going Lightbulb?", Jamie asked him looking at Todd. "I'm great Jamie. Just watching a movie with my lady enjoying the evening."

"Hi Jamie!", Erica smiled.

"Oh tell Erica I said hi.", Jamie replied.

"I can't do this." Todd read Jamie's lips.

"Ooh Erica now that's a fine piece of dark meat", Todd whispered causing Jamie to smile.

"So What's going on Jamie?', Lightbulb asked.

"Well Lightbulb! I have some unpleasant news for you.", Jamie sighed.

"Due to the lack of funding for the fiscal year for our investment company, it will be almost impossible for Todd and I to move forward with the funding of the show."

"WHAT!", Lightbulb replied.

"I'm sorry Lightbulb we will not be funding the show."

"Move me baby!", Lightbulb said standing up then pacing the living room floor bothered and confused.

"What are you saying Jamie? What you mean you're not funding the show?", Lightbulb snapped.

"Sorry man!"

"Wait...wait...wait...wait...wait...wait...wait! We put in a lot of work to get this done—all those meetings man.

Please tell me your joking because this ain't funny at all."

"No Lightbulb this is not a joke man i'm very sorry."

"Buh But Jamie—you know how much this show means to me, my entire career depends on this show.

What am I going to do now? I got some heavy hitters in the music industry that is counting on this show.

The kids and my city is looking forward to this. What i'm going to tell the groups? These kids have nothing man! This is all they have is juking and footworking. You don't know how serious this is man. Where's Todd? let me speak to Todd."

"Hi Lightbulb you're on speaker phone. This was a tough decision but we both came to a consensus on it. I'm sorry man we can't fund the show.", Todd said adding fuel to the fire of Lightbulb's misery.

"We're going to send you a $500 check for all your trouble." "$500", Lightbulb snapped.

"The show costs $50,000!", Lightbulb said while Erica looked worried and concerned.

"Good Luck Lightbulb! That's where its stands. You're check will be in the mail Goodbye!", Jamie said before hanging the phone up.

In disbelief, Lightbulb looked at Erica then burying his face into the palms of his hands.

"FUCK!", Lightbulb hollered startling Erica.

"Baby What Happened?", Erica asked. In their 5 years together, Erica had never seen Lightbulb so upset. Trying to comfort him, Erica wrapped her arms around his back.

"Not right now Erica!", Lightbulb said shrugging his shoulder moving away from her.

"Dirty no good WHITE MOTHERFUCKAS!", Lightbulb snapped.

"My uncle use to always tell me never trust a white motherfucka. They're not gonna finance the show the babe."

"Why?", Erica asked.

"Some bullshit about not getting their finances right for the fiscal year.",Lighbulb snapped.

"What am I gonna do now? They tell me a week before I need to have the fucking money in.", Lightbulb said.

"The show is 4 fucking weeks away. I got every radio station in Chicago talking about. I got these dance groups all ready for the show. Chris Brown and Ciara's managers are gonna be there not to mention Chris Brown and Ciara's gonna be there themselves in person.", Lightbulb said venting and stressing out.

Lightbulb slipped on his jeans. Threw on a shirt and grabbed his car keys.

"Where you going?"

"I don't know Erica!", Lightbulb said slamming the condos door.

Her eyes tight and worried, Erica stared at the door.

While Lightbulb was receiving the bad news about the show, the ambulance crew were performing CPR on Aniya as she lay lifeless on a stretcher being rushed through the doors of the emergency area at Advocate Trinity Hospital with Lemon and her mom following behind. Greeted by 3 surgeons and 2 nurses, the Ambulance crew explained her situation as they rushed into ICU.

"We gotta 9 year old black female with 2 gunshot wounds to the upper body. She's unresponsive. Her heartbeat is low, but we got her breathing again."

They rushed Aniya into surgery stopping Lemon and her mom from following any further.

"That's my baby!", Aniya's mom hollered fighting with the hospital staff. Fortunately the hospital security was able to calm her down.

"I'm sorry mam! We can't let you in."

"But that's my baby!", She cried hysterically full of unsettling emotions.

"I understand mam, but don't worry their gonna do everything in their power to save her.", The male nurse explained.

"Come with me.", He said walking Aniya's mom and Lemon to the hospital's waiting room.

Crying and hugging each other, Lemon and her mom sat on the couch.

Back in the operating room, A trauma team of nurses, surgeons, anastesiologists, surgery techs, and doctors immediately strapped on rubber gloves and went to work on Aniya.

"Stay with us Angel", one of the nurses said gently rubbing Aniya's soft small hand, before whispering a short prayer to God. Surgery techs and nurses poked her small fragile arms with needles hooking her up to IV's and heart monitors.

"We need to open her lungs. There is intense bleeding around her lungs.", One of the head surgeons told the team. Right before a nurse was about to inject Aniya with medicine, a surgeon stopped her.

"NO WAIT!", He shouted.

"What is her weight estimation?"

"68 pounds", Someone shouted.

There was no time to discipline the nurse, but she knew she was in big trouble. Weight estimation is an important part of managing trauma in children because an inaccurate dosng of medicine may be critical. The dosage the nurse had prepared would have killed Aniya. The nurse didn't mean any harm. She just reacted impulsively trying to save Aniya's life. Another nurse with the correct dosage injected Aniya's arm with a needle. Incuated with a mask device, a tube was secured on Aniya's face connected to a T-piece and breathing circuit.

"Stay with us Angel", A head surgeon said before making an incision in Aniya's chest. Sedated, Aniya was barely clinging to life. She was hooked up to a mechanical ventilator. The machine was monitoring her vital organs and stabilizing her condition for surgery.

The chance of survival for the level one trauma patient decreases significantly after an hour has passed.

"Blood pressure is low, critical injury score is a .5", One of the surgeons panicked. Then suddenly the heart monitor went flatline. Aniya's heart stopped. Aniya's chest was open so a surgeon had to use his two fingers to literally pump Aniya's heart.

"Come on baby stay with us.", one of the surgeons panicked. Surprisingly through it all, Aniya had a smile on her beautiful face.

"How long before the Golden hour is over?", One doctor asked his nurse.

"Two minutes!", She panicked.

Chapter 19

Thanksgiving Day at the Williams. The delicious aroma of sweet yams, honey ham, macaroni and cheese, apple cornbread, collard greens, peach cobbler, fried chicken, turkey and dressing, cranberry sauce, chocolate and pineapple cakes filled the air of Mr. and Mrs. Williams home.

Mrs. Williams, her daughters and grand daughter had just got done cooking. They were preparing plates for guests, family, and friends for Thanksgiving dinner. Mrs. Williams and Marose couldn't help but notice how distant and strange Lil Bit was acting around Auntie Katherine.

Loading Thanksgiving plates onto the carts, Mrs. Williams looked at Lil Bit before they rolled them out into the dining area.

"Your okay baby!", Mrs. Williams asked her granddaughter.

"I'm okay!", Lil Bit replied.

"Ain't nothing wrong with her.", Auntie Katherine interrupted with a laugh.

"Can't nothing get my neice down. Ain't that right Lil Bit.

Rolling her eyes at Katherine, Lil Bit gave her that don't push me bitch look. The way Lil Bit was feeling was no laughing matter. In fact Auntie Katherine's presence made matters worse. The house was full of relatives, and Marose's and Katherine's childhood friends from the neighborhood. They were having fun drinking, mingling, and listening to old R&B songs.

"There my girls!", Mr. Williams said smiling at Mrs. Williams, Marose, Auntie Katherine, and Lil Bit as they rolled in carts with Thanksgiving dinners on them. After Mrs. Williams and the girls set the tables they sat down at the dining room table. Lil Bit shrugged Auntie Katherine's arm from off of her and hopped up out of her seat after Auntie Katherine tried sitting next to her.

"You're sure okay!",Marose asked sympathetically after Lil Bit took a seat next to her. Lil Bit remained silent. She didn't answer her mom. Concerned, yet waving off the abrupt small confrontation, Mr. Williams decided to continue with the holiday fun.

"Alright Alright Y'awl Quiet down!", Mr. Williams said sitting at the head of the table.

"It's a pleasure to have all y'awl over for thanksgiving dinner.", Mr. Williams said looking at all of their guest.

"A lot of y'awl I've been knowing since you were kids playing with my daughters. I love all y'awl like my own children. And I'm proud of all y'awl. I see some of y'awl grown up to be good young men and women. Look at lil Keith. A Chicago Police officer, I remember when you was nappy head boy chasing after my baby Marose. I thought you was one of these thugs out here but I was wrong. Look at you now, I'm proud of you son."

"Thanks Mr. Williams!", Keith replied."

Let us bless the food.", Mr. Williams said gently touching his wife Mrs. William's hand.

"O' God! We thank you for this earth, our home, for the wide sky and the blessed sun, for the oceans and streams." For those guest who knew Mr. Williams. They knew he could recite some long ass off the subject prayers. Opening their eyes, Marose and Auntie Katherine smiled after reading Keith's lips.

"What the hell oceans and streams have to do with thanksgiving dinner", Keith whispered causing Marose and Katherine to chuckle. Mr. Williams continued.

"We thank you for our senses by which we hear the songs of birds, and see the splendor of fields of golden wheat, and taste autumn's fruit rejoice in the feel of snow, and smell the breath of spring flowers." Athough Keith grew up to be a Chicago Police Officer, he was still the same mischief lil boy the girls known all of their lives, he had to hold in his laughter.

"Lord thank you for our friends and guest.", Mr. Williams continued with his eyes close unaware that the majority of his was secretly laughing at him."

"Thank you for our children. Bless them with your love and peace. Protect them with your truth and strength, engage them with your hope and vision. Thank you for the food that nourish our bodies. In Jesus name Amen!"

Mr. Williams opened his eyes confused looking at the peculiar faces wondering why they had half smiles on their faces.

"Let's eat!",Mr. Williams said causing a few people to laugh only God knows why?

While everyone dug into their plates, Playing with her food Lil Bit looked sad.

"What's wrong with you girl?",Marose asked frustrated and worried. When tears began to form in Lil Bit's eyes, Marose knew it was serious. Shaking her head, a tear ran down Lil Bit's face.

"I can't do it no more mom!", Lil Bit whispered.

"Do what girl? What are you talking about?", Marose asked looking around hoping no one was looking, but in fact, a few faces were watching them including Auntie Katherine.

"I don't want Grandma to die. But I just can't do it no more mom", Lil Bit said this time a little louder catching everyone's attention.

"What are you talking about girl?", Marose asked. Now with the entire house quieting down focusing their full attention on Lil Bit. Bursting out in tears, Lil Bit released her pain.

"I'm sorry Grandma!", Lil Bit cried.

"You didn't do nothing to me baby!", Mrs. Williams replied with concern worried about her grandbaby's sudden outburst.

Sobbing and crying, Lil Bit continued.

"You being sick with cancer and papa losing the house, I was doing what family was suppose to do for each other, But I just can't do it no more Grandma.", Lil Bit cried.

Mrs. Williams got up from her chair and walked over to Lil Bit then wrapped her arms around her.

"It's okay baby.", she said hugging her."I'm not sick."

"Losing the house!", Mr. Williams added.

"We own this house."

Shaking her head no from side to side, Auntie Katherine stared at Lil Bit from across the table.

"I don't got cancer sweetie. Who told you that?", Mrs. Williams asked.

"They stink and their nasty!", Lil Bit snapped with her face now wet from tears as the house got quieter than a church mouse. All eyes were on Lil Bit.

Lil Bit pointed at Auntie Katherine.

"Auntie Katherine told me that!", Lil Bit cried.

"You go fuck them mothafuckas I ain't no hoe Bitch!", Lil Bit snapped.

"Go find somebody else to be your hoe and prostitute for you!"

The cat was out of the bag. The truth was out. For two years, since Lil Bit was 14 years old, Auntie Katherine has been prostituting her own niece out to strange men. Mr. Williams, Mrs. Williams, Marose and the entire house were in shock from what they just heard.

"What?",Marose snapped at Auntie Katherine.

"You did what?", Marose snapped as she charged at Auntie Katherine like a linebacker knocking Katherine out of her chair then tackling her to the floor throwing a fury of punches to her face.

"You did what to my baby you trifling bitch!", Marose screamed as she punched and scratched Katherine's face. Rocking and cradling Lil Bit in her arms, Mrs. Williams consoled her grieving and crying daughter.

"It's gonna be okay baby!", Mrs. Williams cried.

"I did it for you Grandma!", Lil Bit cried in her Grandmother's arms.

Meanwhile, Mr. Williams and a few men pulled at Marose, trying to get her off of Katherine's ass.

"I'm a kill you Bitch!", Marose screamed as Mr. Williams and the men tried calming her down.

"Please stop Marose! Stop it now girl!", Mr. Williams demanded.

"Bitch you had my daughter prostituting. Let me go daddy!", Marose said. She was out of control.

"I said stop Marose!"

Dazed, hair messy, and bleeding scratches on her face, Auntie Katherine staggered to her feet as Marose stared at her in rage;

"Where's my phone?", Marose asked looking around pointing at Katherine.

"I'm calling the police on you BITCH!" Family and guest didn't know what to do? Should they intervene and try to console the family during this difficult time or should they wait until everybody is back in their right minds. They were shocked. This wasn't the time to take sides, the family and guest loved the Williams's. Katherine and all, If anything the family need their love and support. In an instance, Marose anger turned into sadness as she dropped head. How could her own sister do that to her daughter. "You're supposed to be my sister? How could you do this to my daughter", Marose cried. Now it all makes since to Marose, she knew something was wrong with her daughter.

Chapter 20

While sitting in his car in front of Meechie's dope house, Lightbulb started his car up ready to drive away. As bad as he didn't want to ask Meechie for the money to finance the show, he knew that he had no other choice. So he turned his car off and dialed Meechie's cell phone number.

"What's up Lightbulb?",Meechie answered.

"I'm downstairs Fam!", Lightbulb responded heavy with the sound of distress in his voice and tone.

He was still in shock about how those bitch ass investors played him. For some time now, Meechie wanted to invest in something with Lightbulb. Now was his chance. Meechie's lil cousin Willie lets Lightbulb into the trap house.

Shirtless sporting a gold chain around his neck wearing army fatigue cargo pants and army fatigue slippers with a blunt in his mouth, Meechie walks into the living room clutching the neck of a bottle of hennessy in his hand. Wearing a sarcastic smurk on his face, Meechie shook his head.

"Fucking with them white motherfucka's", Meechie laughed as he took a seat next to Lightbulb. Speechless and full of shame feeling the agony of defeat, Lightbulb dropped his head and took a deep breath shaking his head then lifting it back up making eye contact with Meechie.

"Yeah! It's all bad fam", Lightbulb replied feeling the pain.

"I hate seeing you like this Bulb!", Meechie said stretching out his arm.

"Here hit this. This will calm you're nervous."

"Naw I'm good!"

"Hit the blunt nigga!", Meechie insisted.

"Get that shit off your mind you're with me now. I got you fam."

It was the first time in 3 years since Lightbulb hit some weed. Taking a few puffs, his amateur lungs couldn't withstand the potent loud weed causing him to cough hysterically.

"You're alright man!", Meechie said walking to the kitchen to retrieve some glasses. He poured Lightbulb and himself some hennessy.

"You gotta be careful with that shit. That's that Loud.",Meechie said sitting down.

"Fuck with your own people next time. Fucking them white boys ain't about shit but don't trip fammo I got you."

"I hear you Meech man!"

"I'm glad you came to fuck with me fam.", Meechie said leaving the living room.

"I got the 50 racks right here in the bedroom. You must be a real nigga for me to give you 50 G's.", Meechie laughed a sinister chuckle coming back into the living room with a gym bag full of money throwing it in Lightbulb's lap.

"I really respect you Lightbulb"

"Thanks Meech man!", Lightbulb said looking at all the money inside the bag feeling a sense of relief.

"I hate I had to come ask you. But this big juke show is gonna make at least 150 thousand dollars.

I really appreciate this Meechie man. You don't got nothing to worry about fam. I'm a have all your money plus interest.", Lightbulb reassured him.

"You gon be right there with me man. Chris Brown and Ciara is gonna be in the building. A bunch of record executives—it's gon be cracking. You helped out a lot of people Meech. You gotta good heart man.", D.J. Lightbulb said showing his gratitude.

"Thanks Lightbulb! You know I've been down with you since day one.",Meechie replied.

"But I do need one favor from you. I wouldn't ask you to do something I wouldn't do myself."

"What's that Meech? Anything Fam.", Lightbulb replied. Lowkey he knew it was too good to be true that he could just walk out of Meechie's spot with 50 G's without him wanting nothing in return.

Leaning in, Lightbulb was all ears.

"I need you to ride to Minnesota with this Bitch for me man. It's all good, but it's better to be safe than sorry and I trust you more than that bitch. You know what I mean?—it'sgon be 5 bricks dipped in the car. I already got the money from my people up there. You don't gotta exchange or meet nobody. All you doing is dropping the car off and I got you and that bitch first class flights back to Chicago. It's that easy I do it all the time.",Meechie explained.

"It's all good Meech man!", Lightbulb said before taking shot of hennessy then looking Meechie squarely in his eyes.

"Whatever you want I got you? I'm happy you was able to do this for me fam.", Lightbulb said as he stood up throwing the money bag strap over his shoulder.

"Thanks a lot Bro!", Lightbulb said giving Meechie a bro hug.

"In this game you can't trust no one. But we go way back. I trust you with my life. I'm glad I could help.", Meechie said walking Lightbulb to the door.

"Aye!",Meechie said to Lightbulb right before he left out the door.

"I just wanted to tell you be careful around here with all that money—niggas thirsty ass fuck out here."

"I'm Good Meech man! Good looking Tho! See you in a few days.", Lightbulb said before he leaving Meechie's spot.

Chapter 21

One week and three surgeries later, Aniya was still in critical condition. After endless hours of crying and praying in the hospitals waiting room, day and night, Lemon and her mom kept their faith in God that Aniya will make a full recovery. They hadn't spoken to any nurse, surgeon, or doctor in the past 8 hours. They grew impatient and worried. They were eagered to find out what was going on with Aniya.

Sway, Auriel, and Lil Bit walks into the waiting room;

"Hi Ms. Hamilton", Sway said as she greeted Lemon's mom hugging her for a few seconds longer showing her sincere sympathy and affection.

"Hey Baby!", Ms. Hamilton replied. The pain and agony affected her usual soft voice. Sway looked at Lemon.

"How is she?", Sway asked.

"She had surgery last night, but we haven't heard nothing since last night.", Lemon explained.

"She's gonna be okay Lemon.", Sway said giving Lemon a hug.

"My mom's church been praying for Aniya and the whole hood been praying for her. My baby boo is going is gonna make it. Prayer works."

"Thanks Sway!"

Looking at Auriel and Lil Bit, Sway looked at Lemon.

"Can I talk to you Lemon!", Sway asked.

"Yeah!", Lemon replied following Sway, Auriel, and Lil Bit into the hospital's hallway. "Be right back mom!"

"What's up Sway?", Lemon asked.

"Lemon!", Sway said taking a deep breath.

"I know this ain't the right time boo, but you're still gonna do the show with us right?"

"Are you fucking serious Sway?", Lemon snapped.

"My baby sister is in there fighting for her life and you're worried about a fucking juke show! Who does that?"

"That's my baby sister too Lemon!", Sway replied getting defensive. "You, Aury, and Lil Bit—all y'awl are my sisters. You know how much I love Aniya. And I know she's gonna make it. But we gotta do this show regardless. We gotta do this show for us. We gotta do this show for Aniya!"

"Sway!", Lemon said throwing her hands up.

"I'm not even thinking about a fucking show right now. Ok! I don't want to talk about it no more.", Lemon said as she walked back into the waiting room leaving Sway, Auriel, and Lil Bit in the hallway looking distraught as a gang of nurses, doctors, and a chaplain walked pass them then into the waiting room where Lemon and her mom was sitting.

From her experience of working in the hospital, Ms. Hamilton knew that the site of a chaplain along with doctors and nurses to give an update about a love one's condition was a bad sign. The nurses and doctors surrounded Lemon and her mom. Their serious demeanor didn't look to good.

"We tried our best Ms. Hamilton.", One of the nurses said. "And it worked out well. Aniya is gonna be fine."

Standing speechless with her right hand covering her mouth, Ms. Hamilton eyes lit up as bright as the sun. Tears of joy watered her eyes as pearl-shaped tears rolled down her cheeks. Without saying a word, Ms. Hamilton bear hugged the nurse.

"Oh thank You!", Ms. Hamilton cried.

"Thank you so much. Thank you Jesus!", Ms. Hamilton celebrated lifting her arms to the sky causing Lemon and the hospital staff to smile with joy.

"Surgery was a success. She's still in serious condition, but she's stabilized and she's doing much better. You have a very strong little girl. We moved her out of ICU and she has a room now. She's been up for about 20 minutes. Right now she's watching the powerpuff girls.", The doctor smiled.

"Can we see her", Aniya's mom asked.

"Of course you can!", The doctor replied.

"The hospital staff is in there changing her beddings and as soon as their done. The nurse Trish will come out to get you."

Ecstatic and joyful, Ms. Hamilton and Lemon smiled as they hugged each other celebrating the good news. Sway, Auriel, and Lil Bit overheard the doctors conversation before they approached Ms. Hamilton and Lemon. In less than 60 seconds, the emotions in the waiting room went from dreadfully weary to ecstatically joyful, happy, and hopeful.

As promised, Trish the nurse walks back into the waiting room to take Ms. Hamilton, and the girls to go see Aniya. With all smiles and tears of joy, Ms. Hamilton and the girls followed the nurse into Aniya's room. Slightly adjusted upwards in the bed with an IV in her arm, and an ekg machine monitoring her vital signs, Aniya was watching the powerpuff girls.

"Ba–By!", Ms. Hamilton cried gently embracing and kissing Aniya then rubbing her hair softly.

"Hi Mommy!", Aniya slurred.

"Oh Ba–by! Hi ya doing?", Ms. Hamilton cried as she gently embraced Aniya happy to hear her voice again. Standing on each side of Aniya's bed— Lil Bit, Sway, Auriel, and Lemon looked at Aniya touching her small hands and arms. She was surrounded by love.

"Hi Lemon!", Aniya smiled at her big sister.

"Hey girl!", Lemon cried unable to fight her tears.

"Mommy, I saw God and I didn't want to leave him. It smelled so good in his house. He was the most prettiest person I ever saw. He was even finer than Chris Brown.", Aniya spoke softly causing the girls to laugh. "God is Fine! He is beautiful", Aniya said seriously.

"I'm happy God gave you back to me Aniya!", Ms. Hamilton smiled crying uncontrollably.

"I made God smile Mommy."

"You did! How baby?"

"I told God that my sister Lemon and her friends are the best juke dancers in my neighborhood. And he said show me! And I start juking for him and he start smiling.", Aniya explained. A nurse and a doctor walks into Aniya's room.

"Hi Sweetie!", The nurse said to Aniya. The doctor turned to Ms. Hamilton.

"I'm sorry. I'm a have to ask you all to leave. We need to run some more test on her. But she's doing great!", The doctor explained.

"Ms. Hamilton, I really need for you to go home and get you some rest. Aniya is okay now. She's doing much better. She's in the healing process now. And because she's so young she's going to make a full recovery. You have a very strong little girl. So please.

Take your other daughter home and y'all get y'awl some rest.

The worst is over."

As bad as Ms. Hamilton didn't want to leave Aniya at the hospital, for the first time in a week, Ms. Hamilton considered taking the doctor's advice and go home. Hearing Aniya speak and seeing her smile again was the greatest gift Ms. Hamilton and the girls could ever receive. Ms. Hamilton leaned over Aniya's hospital bed railing.

"Love you baby! Mommy is gonna go home and get your favorite teddy bears and balloons and I'm a bring your friend Samiah too." "Love you too mommy."

"Love you Aniya!", Lemon, Sway, Auriel, and Lil Bit said before they left her room.

Chapter 22

Sitting in the offices of Billions Boys entertainment company, and across from the company's president, Lightbulb was edgy, frantic, nervous, stressed, and worried. He was minutes away from handing over the $35,000 cashier's check to seal the deal for the huge Juke Contest. Just two more forms to sign and the show was officially ready to move forward. For the most part of the day, Lightbulb had been running around Chicago like a chicken with his head cut off. The radio and T.V. ads were for paid for. He met picked up Chris Brown and Ciara's managers from O'hare's airport. And now he was conducting his last errand of the day. The company's president couldn't help from noticing how tense and strange Lightbulb was behaving. Someone was blowing his cell phone up and for the entire meeting every few seconds, Lightbulb was checking his phone. The company's president couldn't wait to get his nervous wreck ass out of his office. But Lightbulb had every reason to be nervous and antsy. He fucked up. He fucked up bad. He didn't do the drug run to Minnesota for Meechie and to make matters worse, the girl Meechie sent to Minnesota ran off with 10 of bricks of his cocaine. All 100 texts and missed calls were from Meechie. Lightbulb was eagered to end the meeting, so he could get home quick fast and a hurry to Erica. The only reason, he kept his phone on was to hear from Erica to make sure she was safe.

"Sorry for the phone!", Lightbulb said nervously.

"My girl's pregnant and you know how that is.

She probably got one of those pregnant cravings for a pickle and a hot fudge sundae and want me to pick it up. It can't be an emergency she's only 5 months pregnant. So I know she's not about to have the baby!", Lightbulb lied making up a story.

"Those pregnant women!", Lightbulb laughed signing the last form. Standing to his feet, Lightbulb leaned over the desk.

"So we're good?", He asked.

"Uh! Yeah it's all good.", The Company's President said checking the paper work.

"You understand the stipulations.

You're business and marketing plan looks good.

The papers are signed. So Yes! It's official", He said shaking Lightbulb's hand.

"Well I guess you gotta get home to you're wife."

"Sure do! And thanks again Mr. Conner.", Lightbulb said as he rushed out of his offices walking fast to his car. Lightbulb hopped in then took off; Speeding thru traffic listening to Meechie's voice messages over speaker phone, Lightbulb had every reason to be worried.

"FUCK!", Lightbulb slammed his hand onto the steering wheel waiting at the traffic light after Erica's phone went to voicemail for the 3rd time. Then his phone rings. Dreading to answer it, he mustered up the balls to answer it.

"Hello!"

"What's up man?"

"Derrick?", Lightbulb asked.

"Yeah! What's up man?"

"Oh hey Derrick, What's up?" Derrick was Ciara's and Chris Brown manager.

"I was just calling you to fill you in with some good news. I spoke to Ciara earlier today and I just got off the phone with Chris and their both excited about the show. They say they love coming to Chicago. They got so much love there."

"Fa sho Derrick that's what's up man! Yo Derrick. I just made it to the crib. Let me get at you later on Bro."

"No Worries Lightbulb. I was just keeping you posted bro. See you in 2 weeks.", Derrick said before he hung the phone up. After D.J. Lightbulb pulled up to his crib, he parked his car and hopped out. Running upstairs he busted into his Condo.

"Erica!", He said walking thru his crib dreading the worse.

"Erica!"

"Baby What's wrong?", Erica said wearing a bath robe just getting out of the shower.

"Oh Baby!", D.J. Lightbulb said hugging her. Grabbing her by her shoulders, he looked squarely into her eyes.

"Erica! Listen to me. I need for you to go to your mother's house today."

"Why Baby?", Erica said with concern sensing the urgency in Lightbulb's deamenor.

"Please baby just do it. I will explain to you later. Just get your t h i n g s and go to your mom's house today. Like now!"

"What's going on?", Erica asked.

"Does this have to do with those crazy calls I've been getting?"

"What calls?"

"Someone just called here three times and didn't say a word. I was saying hello! hello! hello!, but no reponse. I heard a T.V. in the background."

Looking out of their living room window at cars and people searching for anything or anyone suspicious, Lightbulb stayed calmed making sure he wouldn't startle Erica, but he was scared as hell.

"Baby!", He exhaled deeply with the look of distress on his face.

"I will explain everything later. Just get your things now and go to your mama's house. Please baby Hurry!"

"I'm scared baby. What's going on?", Erica said. It was no laughing matter, but Lightbulb wanted to say he was scared to; but he kept his cool. "Are you gonna be ok!" Erica asked. "Yes!", He snapped."

Now Get ready!", Lightbulb hollered.

Meanwhile, pulling up to D.J. Lightbulb's condominiums, one of Meechie's goons call Meechie's cell phone;

"Yo! Meech. Is that address 2139 Michigan, in those brown buildings?"

"yeah that's it."

"You said he gotta black Maxima right."

"Yep!"

"Aight Bet Fam, I see it out here. It's all good, I'm a holla at you later.", One of Meechie's hitters said before he hung up his phone. Looking for an inconspicuous parking space across from D.J. Lightbulb's building, the driver of the old school black chevy impala with tinted windows found a parking spot. Three of Meechie's goons sat patiently in the impala waiting for D.J. Lightbulb.

Back upstairs in Lightbulb's condo, every few seconds he peeped out of the window every few seconds.

"Come on.", Lightbulb said to Erica as she walks into the living room with 2 louievutton bags filled with clothes. D.J. Lightbulb gently palmed Erica's face in his hands.

"Baby I'm a come over to your mama's in a few hours and explain everything to you. I promise. I love you baby now come on.", D.J. Lightbulb said as he grabbed Erica's bags as they walked out of their condo. Afraid and confused, Erica followed Lightbulb to her car.

"Click" Meechie's goons unlocked their doors when they noticed Erica and Lightbulb walking to her car. Locked and loaded, they were about to shoot shit up. Right before their feet touched the street pavement, loud blaring sirens went off as paramedics, fire trucks, and police cars sped past their car. Looking at all the commotion, D.J. Lightbulb threw Erica's luggage in her trunk then walked her to the driver's side of her car as she got in.

"I'm a be there in a few hours.", D.J. Lightbulb said before kissing her and shutting the driver's door. Sitting teary eyed in her seat wondering if that was the last time she'll ever see Lightbulb again, Erica drove away. D.J. Lightbulb ran back into the building. The goons watched as Erica's car passed by them from the opposite side of the street.

Chapter 23

After sitting in the car for 2 hours in front of D.J. Lightbulb's condo building, Meechie's goons were growing impatient.

"Let's just run up in there and murk this motherfucka.", The tallest one of Meechie's goons said to the others.

"Hell Yeah! I feel you fam.", The goon in the driver's seat replied as he redialed Meechie's phone number on his cell.

"Whaddup?", Meechie answered his phone.

"Aye Meech man! Were still out here waiting on ya boy. It looks like this motherfucker ain't coming back out here. Gimme the word and we up there."

"Calm down my nigga! I've been thinking fam. Y'all don't have to kill that nigga, just give him that seven tray, give him anotha few hours. If you don't see the motherfucka by then we'll just get at him another time."

"Alright Bet!", The goon in the driver's seat replied then hung up the phone. Moments after he hung up his cell phone, Lightbulb walked out of his building carrying a gym bag heading towards the middle of the street by the driver's side of his vehicle.

"Let's go!", The goons said hopping out of their Chevy ready to handle their business. It happened so fast. Right before Lightbulb even noticed them, they were right before his eyes a few feet away rushing towards him; he didn't even have enough time to react. The only connection Lightbulb made right before the goons gave him that 73rd street beat down was when he swung his gym bag smacking one of the goons in his face. D.J. Lightbulb stood his ground for a few seconds, before getting overpowered by the fury of punches and kicks the goons delivered to his face and body. Glass shattered on the driver's side of Lightbulb's car from the impact of his head getting shoved through it. Lighbulb's body flopped to the ground. They kicked Lightbulb until half of his body was wedged underneath his car.

"MOTHERFUCKA!", The tallest one of the goons said giving Lightbulb one good last kick. They ran back to the Chevy. Hopped in then sped away. Out cold, Lightbulb's body was stuck underneath his car. Walking in the middle of the street, A group of teenagers walking in the middle of the street noticed Lightbulb's body stuck underneath his car.

"Oh Shit!", one of the teenagers said opening his arms stopping his friends.

"Is he dead?"

"I don't know!", the other teenager said to the other. If it wasn't for one of the teenagers in the Chicago bulls cap, a car would've ran over Lightbulb's arm and leg. Springing into action waving his arms frantically, the teenager in the bulls cap ran in front of the car. "Wait...Wait...Wait...Wait!", He hollered. Slamming on his breaks, the driver swerved away from Lightbulb's body nearly running over him and crashing into a parked car. The driver got out of his car and saw Lighbulb's body in the street wedged under his car. "Is he dead?", The driver asked the teenagers. "No. Look!", One of the teenagers replied.

"He's breathing!" Shortly before the driver got on his phone and called for help, a small crowd of onlookers looked over Lightbulb as he lay out cold badly injured. Finally the ambulance came and took him to the hospital.

Chapter 24

Meechie's boys fucked Lightbulb up really bad. Laying in the hospital bed, he had suffered a fractured eye socket, a mild concussion, bruised kidney, and a broken arm. Sitting beside him in a chair his girlfriend Erica rubbed his hand. Awakening suddenly after 10 days of operations and heavy sedation, the first thing Lightbulb asked for was his cellphone. "What's today?", Lightbulb slurred surprising Erica.

"Bae!", Erica replied. "You're talking babe."

"Yeah! Yeah!", Lightbulb moaned. "What's today?"

"It's March 25th"

"March 25th!"

"Yes Babe"

"What time is it?"

"It's 9:30 in the morning."

"I need my cellphone. Where's my cellphone?", Lightbulb said as he moaned in pain and agony.

"Right here! Why?", Erica responded.

"I gotta meet with Chris Brown and Ciara's Manager at 2 o'clock. The show is tomorrow night!", Lightbulb said as he listened to one of his voicemail messages.

Chapter 25

Although the crowd cheered after the Ladies of Action dance performance, the girls were frustrated. It was a disaster. From the time the girls met with D.J. Lightbulb in the dressing room seeing him wearing sunglasses covering a black eye and wearing a cast on his broken arm, they felt discouraged. When the girls asked him.

What happened to him? And he replied nothing just an accident, instantly they knew something bad had happened. The D.J. that Lightbulb had hired wasn't playing the right music. Now they were discouraged, frustrated and unsure of themselves in front of Chris Brown, Ciara, producers, BET, and thousands of people. And to make matters worse, Lemon was becoming sick and tired from being 4 months pregnant out there trying to Juke.

"I don't feel good!", Lemon told Auriel, Lil Bit, and Sway as they were walking off the stage heading back towards the dressing rooms.

"My feet is killing me. It feel like I'm about to faint."

"FUCK!", Sway snapped as she plopped down onto the couch exhausted from dancing frowning as her eyes pierced at Lemon.

"I hate your ass Lemon. How we gon win now?", Sway snapped.

"Calm down girls!", D.J. Lightbulb interrupted.

"Y'awl is doing good out there you heard them cheering like crazy for y'awl. They went crazy for y'awl. They love you girls out there."

"Buh but Lightbulb. How we gon win? And make it to the last round.", Sway complained.

"Those bitches is killing us out there. All the work we put in!", Sway cried becoming emotional voice crackling with emotion. Auriel and Lemon watched on feeling defeated with tears forming in their eyes. Even Lightbulb had his doubts. Although, he wanted the best for all of the groups participating in the show, it was something about Sway, Auriel, Lemon, and Lil Bit that made him believe in them. Especially Lil Bit, he's thrown 100's of shows and watched thousands of dancers dance, but he had never in his life seen no one as good as Lil Bit. She danced with so much passion. Like Michael Jordan, Lebron James, and Kobe Bryant—she was carrying the team. She was carrying the girls. While the girls argued, fussed, and was feeling defeated. Lil Bit was focused and determined to win.

"I'm sorry Sway!", Lemon cried hugging Sway.

"AND THE LADIES OF ACTION!", One of the judges announced over the loud speakers—shocking and catching the girls off guard, they looked at each other.

"WHAT?", Auriel hollered. If the girls were listening, they would have heard over the speakers that they had just made it to the last rounds of dancing, defeating out 6 other dance groups.

"What they say?", Sway smiled yet in disbelief.

"Y'awl made it to the last round!", Lightbulb replied.

Jumping up and down, Auriel and Lil Bit screamed. In an instance, the girls went from hopeless and defeated to hopeful and optimistic. Tears turned into joy. Frowns turned into smiles.

"Yes girl we made it", LiL Bit hollered celebrating with Sway, Lemon and Auriel. Fearless Squad, Notorious Diamonds, and the Ladies of Action have made it to the last round.

The intermission was coming to an end. Stuck and still celebrating and staring at each other in the faces with smiles on their faces, the girls didn't know what to do?

"Go out there! Y'awl gotta go out there!", Lightbulb said laughing estatic for the girls. Sway, Auriel, Lemon, and Lil Bit ran on stage. Lil Bit waved at her Mom Marose, who was in the crowd jumping and hollering with Mr. and Mrs. Williams beside her. Nervous and looking at the hundreds of people in the crowd, the girls stood next to Fearless Squad, and the Notorious Diamonds. After the crowd cheered for the groups, the D.J. congratulated the girls, the girls walked off stage back to their dressing rooms. Fearless squad was up next to dance. From start to finish, Fearless Squad has been juking their asses off. Those bitches were blazing the stage giving the other dance groups the business and The Ladies of Action and The Notorious Diamonds knew this. They knew that they had to do something, because Fearless Squad has been winning the whole dance competition.

Back in the dressing room, the good news of advancing to the last round and the excitement was fading away. It was back to business for the L.O.A Girls, Fearless Squad, and The N-otorious Diamonds. They each beat out 3 other groups and had made it to the last round, but now they gotta win it all. The best group wins. Changing into their sexy sheer lacy stand out style and flawless red dance outfits still happy as hell chatting, and giggling with each other, Sway noticed Lemon sitting quietly on the bench. Feeling bad about screaming on Lemon 15 minutes earlier, Sway took a seat next to Lemon wrapping her arm around her.

"I'm sorry girl", Sway said hugging Lemon's shoulder.

"When we get back to hood, I'm cooking you your favorite Lasagna just for you. You know I gotta feed you my nephew cooking in your belly.", Sway smiled as she rubbed Lemon's pregnant stomach. However, Sway word's seemed to not move Lemon. Still sitting in a daze, a tear ran down Lemon's cheek. For a girl whose group that just made it to the last round for a chance to win $50,000, Lemon sure wasn't acting like she was happy.

"What's wrong girl?", Sway asked.

"I can't dance no more", Lemon cried.

"Huh! What?", Sway replied.

"I can't do it no more girl, my fucking feet is killing me. My whole body hurts. It feels like I'm a faint out there. I'm sorry y'all.", Lemon cried sniffing as tears rolled down her cheek, face red from crying. Sway, Auriel, and Lil Bit were in shock. They didn't know how to react. They made it this far. Everything mattered at this time and moment. All of their struggles, hard work, and pain lead up to this show. There moments away from dancing in the biggest show of their lives and now their dealt another setback; their girl Lemon can't finish the dance competition. Although, juke music was blasting outside their dressing room, there was an awkward silence among the girls. Then out of nowhere, Lil Bit spoke.

"We can do it!", Lil Bit said breaking the silence.

"Huh!", Auriel replied.

"We don't got no other choice. We can do it. We came this far. I'm not gonna lose!", Lil Bit said with conviction. This means everything to me. If it wasn't for this show, I'll be dead right now. Y'awl know what I went through with my bitch ass Auntie. If I don't go out there and dance, I'm a let that shit destroy me what my own Auntie did to me. And she ain't about to do no more damage to my life. Fuck that I'm not turning back. Juking is my life. It's the only thing that kept me going. Don't worry Lemon. We gon win this for you. We gotta do this for your sister Aniya. We gotta do this for us.", Lil Bit preached with passion and conviction. With serious looks on their faces shaking their heads, Sway and Auriel looked at Lil Bit feeling every bit of word she just said.

"Let's show these motherfucka's who we is and where we come from East Chicago in this Bitch.", Sway snapped. Lightbulb knocked on their dressing room door, before opening it peeping inside.

"Hey y'awl Notorious Diamonds is about to finish. They killing it out there y'awl better bring y'awl A game. Y'all ready?", D.J. Lightbulb asked, noticing Lemon wasn't dressed in the same matching outfits as the rest of the girls.

"What's going on? Why you ain't dressed?", Lightbulb asked Lemon.

"She's good!", Sway replied.

"She can't finish, so it's just gonna be me Auriel, and Lil Bit."

Looking disappointed, shaking his head with no time to respond to the sudden news, Lightbulb left it alone.

"Whatever!", he said disappointedly.

"Y'awl up next; get ready!", D.J. Lightbulb said before shutting the dressing room door.

Back onstage. The crowd gave Notorious Diamonds a standing ovation. Clowning around jumping out of his seat, Chris Brown went nuts. He loved the girls. They killed it. Bowing before the crowd, the Notorious Diamonds dance group was excited and grateful for all the love. They deserved it. They danced their asses off.

"Give it up one more time for the Notorious Diamonds dancers", The replacement D.J. for Lightbulb said into the microphone.

"Those young ladies can dance.", D.J. Turned up said in the microphone.

"Up next these young women have been blazing Chicago for some time now. With their raw talent, street saavy, finesse, and unique style, they made it to the last round. Make some noise for these group of young ladies. THE LADIES OF ACTION! better known as the L.O.A Girls."

Cheering and Hollering, the crowd went crazy for the Ladies of Action.

Before Notorious Diamonds went on stage, D.J. Lightbulb gave the replacement D.J. a special mix he did specifically for Ladies of Action. Back in the dressing room—Sway, Auriel, and Lil Bit were preparing to hit the stage. Forming a circle—Lemon, Lil Bit, Sway, and Auriel held hands.

"This is it!", Sway said to the girls. "Remember what D.J. Lightbulb taught us off that movie."

"Yeah I remember!", Auriel smiled.

"Whose the judge?", Sway asked.

"Oh my God Sway!", Lemon laughed.

"Bitch this ain't the Great Debaters. Who you think you is? The female Denzel Washington""

Just say the damn thing with me. I really like it. It helps me out damn bitch!", Sway said causing Lil Bit and Auriel to laugh and smile.

"Now whose the Judge?", Sway continued before Lemon rudely interrupted her with her smart ass remark.

"The Judge is God!", Lemon, Auriel, and Lil Bit replied.

"Why is he God?"

"Because he decides who wins or loses not my opponent."

"Whose your opponent?"

"He doesn't exist."

"Why does he not exist?"

"Because they are the descending force from the truth we dance", The girls said adding their own little twist to the saying.

"WE THE TRUTH!", The girls said together. Each taking a deep breath the girls were ready to take the stage. Although they were nervous, with their hearts hammering in their chest, the girls were ready. Lemon stopped at the side of the stage as Sway, Auriel, and Lil Bit continued walking out on stage in front of the hundreds of people in the crowd with Chris Brown, Ciara, and Free from 106 and park sitting in the front row, judging the show.

Looking fabulous, beautiful, and sexy in their fishnet stockings showing off their legs and gold and platinum silhouette tights with matching glittering gold and platinum jordans; hairstyles on point with their face made up, the girls looked stunning. Especially Lil Bit, her hair style was attention grabbing with a braid draped over her head. Her long hair was swept up into a huge flawless braid that crowned her head beautifully drawing attention to her facial features. Now center stage in front of what it felt like millions of people—the girls nervously and shyly looked at each other. Standing a foot apart from each other, they looked back at the D.J. signaling to him that they were ready. Auriel glanced at Lemon who was standing by the curtains at the side of the stage giving her a reassuring smile that they were about to kill it. The crowd was silent. Ready for action, the girls bowed their heads as they waited for the music to play. The D.J. clicked play on his laptop.

"Ladies and gentlemen—this is a jazzy fizzle product shizzle!", Ciara's hit song 1,2 step banged loudly through the huge speakers on stage.

Simultaneously, the girls lifted their arms prepping their bodies to dance, before their fancy footwork went into action.

"Rock it don't stop it everybody get on the floor. Crank the party up we're about to get it on. Lemme see you 1,2 step. I love it when you 1,2 step. Everybody 1,2 step we're about to get it on.", The lyrics and music of Ciara's song played with the special mix D.J. Lightbulb put together with a signature juke 808 kick drum and funky snare kick mixed perfectly together. The way the girls were jamming, footworking, and dancing onstage to her song, made Ciara proud putting a huge smile on her face was a good sign. Wide eyed, Free from 106 and park watched in awe as the girls footworked their stuff on stage. After the girls extravagant high powered opening, the bass dropped.

Breathing heavily, the girls froze striking a pose looking into the crowd. The second mix played.

"I'm a-a diva (hey), I'm a, I'm a-a diva (hey) I'm a, I'm a-a diva (hey)", The computerized chipmunk voice played mix with Beyonce repeating (hey)

"Na-na-na, diva is a female version of a hustla, of a hustla, of a, of a hustla... Na-na-na, diva is a female version of a hustla, of a hustla, of a, of a hustla.

Sway and Lil Bit's backs were turned to the crowd as Auriel stood with her hands on her hips looking like Beyonce in her "Diva" video. Spreading her arms moving her head, neck, and shoulders, Auriel lipsynced Beyonce's rap.

"Stop the track, lemme state facts"

"I told you, gimme a minute and I'll be right back"

Rapping like Beyonce in her Diva video, Auriel continued as Sway and Lil Bit turned around catching the same dance move in perfect harmony with Auriel showing that practice really makes perfect.

"Fifty million 'round the world and they say I couldn't get it"

With their heads back looking up the girls rolled their heads around to the right did a shoulder lean then rolled their upper bodies to the left.

"I got so sick and filthy with Benji's, I can't spend it"

"How you gon be talking shit? You act like I just got up on it"

"Been the number one diva in the game for a minute!", Auriel rapped along with the same energy and rhythm as Beyonce.

After the short Beyonce dance routine, a juke song and pattern mixed in. "PUMP IT, PUMP IT, PUMP IT" repeated 15 times causing the girls to go bezerk with their footwork. Their flying elbows, body jerking, and high energy jumping made the crowd stand up and cheer. With passion, determination, and high energy, the girls danced like their lives were on the line. Flawlessly, their dance moves fit the lyrics and beats to the juke mix.

Each set of moves flowed easily to the next set of moves. Their dance routine was so good, people in the crowd start busting out their video cameras, smartphones and began videotaping them. Finishing strong, the girls went out with a bang bringing down the house. Hearts pounding in their chest, breathing heavily, striking fierce poses, the girls held hands bowing before the crowd of screaming people.

"That's my baby...that's my baby!", Lil Bits mom Marose hollered crying and jumping up and down with excitement. Standing beside her Lil Bit's granddaddy Mr. Williams had to grab Marose to calm her down.

"Alright alright alright!, Ladies and gentlemen that was Chicago's very own Ladies of Action", Lightbulb's replacement D.J. Turn up said into the Microphone leaning over.

"Give it up one more time for these young women out here snapping. I thought that was Beyonce rapping for a minute. Lil mama got off Didn't she?", D.J. Turned up laughed. With wide smiles on their faces, cheesing from ear to ear the girls galloped off stage where they met up with Lemon by the stage curtains.

"Y'awl Bitches killed it!", Lemon said animatedly with a huge smile on her face. "Auriel girl you killed that Beyonce rap. I videotaped yo ass! I'm a call your ass Sasha Fierce Now.", Lemon laughed.

"I thought I was off for a minute until I saw Lil Bit and Sway snapping they got me geeked.", Auriel said laughing and celebrating with her bitches: Lemon, Sway, and Lil Bit as the girls made their way to their dressing room. Standing in the hallway a few yards away by their dressing room door, the Notorious Diamond dancers were giving the Ladies of Action dirty looks.

"Fake Bitches can't even dance.", One of the Notorious Diamonds girls said loud enough that Sway, Lemon, Auriel, and Lil Bit could hear it. Lemon turned around and rolled her neck ready to swing on the first bitch.

"What you say Hating ass Thot ass Bitches!", Lemon snapped marching towards them with Sway, Auriel, and Lil Bit following behind. Right on time, just before things got ugly. D.J. Lightbulb and his girlfried Erica walked up.

"Girls! Girls! Girls! Calm it down NOW! We ain't about to have this shit going on not today not now not never. If y'awl can't get along, I'm a need y'awl to go back to your dressing rooms. DO YOU UNDERSTAND ME?", D.J. Lightbulb snapped quickly diffusing the situation.

"You gotta show respect for the Next dance group just like they showed respect for you guys", D.J. Lightbulb argued.

Both dance groups nodded their heads after pleading their cases about who started it first then calmly walked back to their dressing rooms.

Back out on stage, D.J. Turned up was announcing the last dance group.

"It's getting Hot in herre so take off all you're clothes, I am getting so Hot I can take my clothes off let's ball out.", D.J. Turned up rapped into the microphone.

"Alright alright! What's up to all my Diva's and Hustlers out there. The ladies are looking good out there. Are y'awl enjoying the show?", D.J. Turned up asked the crowd.

"Maannn! I didn't know this show was gonna be this damn good. I'm sure these next girls will definitely entertain every last one of y'awl. I met these girls last year at the Bud Billiken parade and when I say these girls can dance I mean these girls can dance. They was dope then and their dope now. Representing the Wild Hundreds! Make some noise for the FEARLESS SQUAD!!", D.J. Turned up said stretching the syllables in the group's name. Five of the Fearless Squad dancers ran out on stage in their sexy outfits looking Gorgeous and beautiful. The dancers were ready to turn up. Taking postition, they stood with their arms stretched out and backs turned to the crowd to. The bass drum and the snare kick to Lil Mama's Hit song "Lip Gloss" began to play.

The 6th dancer ran out on stage doing a cartwheel, 2 back flips and a sommersault, right when she landed on her feet, it sounded like a huge explosion vibrating the auditorium startling some of the people in the crowd.

"Lil mama Yeah it's poppin, it's poppin, it's poppin, it's poppin. I gotta ask 'em, 'cause if i don't It's poppin, it's poppin, it's poppin, it's poppin". "What you know 'bout me? What you What you What you know 'bout me? What you know 'bout me? What you What you What you know? They say my lip gloss is cool My lip gloss be popping I'm standing at my locker And all the boys keep stopping" With the same intensity, energy, passion, and confidence as the other groups if not more, the Fearless Squad went in. They footworked moving their bodies to every mix track ranging from "Crank dat Soulja Boy" to Travis Porter "Ayy Ladies" featuring Tyga. Finishing strong, the 6th dancer did 3 more amazing flips like she was the Olympic Champion Gabby Douglas. The rush of excitement and adrenaline rolled over into the crowd causing them to jump up and down celebrating and cheering. From the crowd's reaction, the winners of the show could be any group.

"That was Fearless Squad", D.J. Turned up said into the microphone.

"Aye! What's your name young lady?", D.J. Turned up asked the 6th dancer.

"FE FE!", She replied breathing hard and out of breath.

"FE FE!", D.J.Turned up laughed. "Girl I thought you was gonna flip off stage" His comment made the crowd laugh.

"I'm just joking with you sweetheart. You girls looked real good out there. Give it one more time for Fearless Squad.", D.J. Turned up said busting out laughing.

"Chris Brown jumped out of his seat when Fe Fe did her flips that was too funny."

"I can Flip too", Chris brown hollered out before Ciara handed him a microphone.

"What you say Chris?"

"I said I can flip too!"

"You know Fearless Squad snapped if they got Chris Brown wanting to come up here on stage and do some flips.", D.J. Turned up said bawling his fist then poundin his chess.

"Much Love CB."

Standing at the side of the stage by the curtains, The Ladies of Action, Notorious Diamonds, D.J. Lightbulb and his girlfriend Erica looked on. Stepping down from the D.J. booth, D.J Turned up held the microphone up to his mouth. Speaking into the microphone, he was excited.

"Alright the competition is tight. Each group did the damn thang! Now it's time to announce the winners.", D.J. Turned up said waving for the other groups to come out on stage. Lil Bit pulled Lemon's arm.
"Come on Girl!", Lil Bit said to Lemon as they happily walked out on stage with Lemon following them. Walking behind them, the Notorious Diamonds frowned their faces at the Ladies of Action as they followed behind them. Standing in front of the hundreds of people in the crowd, all of the girls were nervous twiddling their thumbs as some stood pigeion toed. In the V.I.P special seating section in front of the stage—Ciara, Chris Brown, and Free from 106 and park were grouped together whispering to one another. Holding hands, Sway, Auriel, Lil Bit, and Lemon were silently praying for the best outcome, wishing their dream will finally come true. Breaking the huddle up, each celebrity had something to say before Free announced the $50,000 winners.

"First off, I would like to say because of you girls, i'm a new fan of juke and footwork. I ain't never seen no dancing that damn good in a long time. I always tell my people back in Atlanta that Chicago got a lot of talent and you girls proved that tonight.", Ciara said sincerely causing the crowd to applaud her for her feedback.

"Come on Chris, I know you got something to say.", Ciara said to him. "I just wanna say", Chris Brown said with a huge smile on his face. "Shawty, Shawty, She throwing her hair, she working them jeans, She talking that talk just li, li, like I like it, She keep it on and poppin' Oh oh, oh yeah.", Chris Brown sings making all the girls on stage blush and fawn over him.

"Y'awl was poppin, I wish you all could win. I loved all y'awl. I can't wait to have one of y'awl groups dancing in my video. Y'awl gonna have to show me that footwork.", Chris Brown said animatedly.

The girls were cheesing from ear to ear slightly jumping up and down trying to keep their composure. Finally Free announced the winners.

"Like Chris and Ciara said Y'awl girls were amazing and your dancing was phenomenal. The decision was hard.", Free said shaking her head then clutching her heart.

"I wish that all of you girlsl could win but it gots to be only one winner. And the winner is", Free said looking down at the score card.

"THE NOTORIOUS DIAMONDS!", Free hollered. Screaming and shouting for joy, the Notorious Diamond girls hugged one another. One of the Notorious Dancers girls laughed at Lil Bit after Lil Bit Bursted into tears, running off stage.

"Losing ass Bitches!", One of the Notorious Diamond girls said with a smirk on her face to another dancer in her group. Embarrassed and very disappointed, Sway, Auriel, and Lemon stayed on stage enduring the awful upset.

Chapter 26

"Congratulations girls! You did a good job!", D.J. Turned up said to the Notorious Diamonds Dancers before congratulating them by giving each one of them hugs. Shorty afterwards, shaking his head walking over to Sway, Lemon, and Auriel, he gave each one of them hugs too.

"I'm so sorry Girls you girls did a good job today.", D.J. Turned up expressed his concerns as he walked over to Fearless Squad giving them hugs expressing his sorrow for them losing as well followed by giving each Fearless Squad dancer a hug. Neither Ladies of Action nor Fearless Squad congratulated the Notorious Diamonds. They just calmly walked off stage towards their dressing rooms leaving D.J. Turned up and the Notorious Diamonds dancers on stage. Smiling looking arrogant, the Notorious Dancers embraced the moment of winning.

"I be telling bitches, they can't fuck with us.", One of the dancers bragged to the others enjoying thier moment with cheer and laughter.

"Who is that?", Ciara asked Chris Brown and Free pointing at the Notorious Diamonds dancers with a confused look on her face.

"That's the Notorious Diamonds—they're the winners.", Free explained. Burying her head into her hands, Ciara couldn't believe it.

"Oh my God!", Ciara whined. "What?", Chris Brown and Free asked.

"I fucked up Y'awl. I confused the groups. I thought the Notorious Diamonds were the Ladies of Action. Oh my God! I meant to pick The Ladies of Action as the winners", Ciara explained.

"That means me and your votes stands and The Ladies of Action are actually the winners.", Chris Brown replied.

"We gotta let them know!", Free said.

Back in the dressing room, the sound of sadness and disappointment lingered in the air. Lots of crying and sobbing and intakes of breaths with shoulders heaving were happening, the girls were very upset. There were a lot of tears among Auriel, Lemon, Sway and Lil Bit. Sway tried her best to stay strong and comfort a very emotional Lil Bit, but she was just as sad and disappointed as the others.

"It's gonna be ok girl!", Sway cried as she hugged Lil Bit with both arms around her.

"I'm just tired of all this shit!", Lil Bit cried. Erica stopped D.J. Lightbulb from going into the girls dressing room.

"No let me talk to them.", Erica told Lightbulb before knocking on the dressing room's door.

"Can I come in?", Erica asked peeping inside. The sight was heartwrenching for Erica watching the girls cry their hearts out. Rubbing Lil Bit's back, Erica sat down next to her. She had to do something. Unable to speak, short intakes of breath, Lil Bit said the first words that could come out.

"I should have just killed myself long time ago. God No! Oh God No! I can't believe we lost this fucking contest!", Lil Bit cried becoming very emotional. On the other side of the door in the hallway, D.J. Turned up ran up to D.J. Lightbulb.

"Where's your girls?", D.J. Turned up said trying to catch his breath.

"There in the dressing room Why?"

"Fam! Ciara thought that the Notorious Diamonds dancers were your girls man! She made a mistake. Your girls won!"

"You're bullshiting! Stop Playing!", D.J. Lightbulb said in disbelief with slight smile on his face hoping like hell this wasn't a sick joke.

"Do it look like I'm Bullshitting!", D.J. Turned up said with a serious look on his face.

"They just told me. It was a mistake your girls won. They need to come out here."

Back inside of the dressing room—with such warmth, sympathy, and sincerity, Erica definitely felt the girls pain. She remained quiet consoling them for a few moments before speaking. "You girls will always be my favorite dancers", She said embracing the girls with both arms.

"I wish I was like you girls when I was a teenager. You girls are so beautiful, strong, and loyal to each other. Friendship like this is very rare especially in this time of age. Look at you girls. You girls are the true winners."

"Erica this meant everything to us!", Auriel cried.

"I know I know beautiful", Erica said wiping Auriel's face of tears. Let me tell you what my daddy use to tell me—may his soul rest in peace. He use to always tell me. There is nothing in this life that can destroy you but yourself. Bad things happen to everyone, but when they do, you can't fall apart and die. You have to fight back. If you don't you're the one who loses in the end. But if you do keep going and fight back, you win.", Erica explained.

"Girl's it ain't the end of world.", Erica said before getting distracted and interupted by frantic knocks at the door.

"Babe wait! I'm talking to the girls!", Erica shouted.

"No open the door I need to talk to you all it's important.", D.J. Lightbuld said opening the door.

"Come on y'awl!", he said urgently waving his hand. Confused and looking at each other Erica and the girls froze but jumped when Lightbulb hollered.

"NOW! COME ON!", He snapped causing Erica and the girls to jump up like kriss kross and following him out on to the stage in front hundreds of people. Confused wiping their faces of tears, Sway, Auriel, Lemon, and Lil Bit were looking at each other as they stood in front of the hundreds of people in the crowd. With bewildered expressions on their faces, the girls looked at the judges.

"Hi Girls!", Ciara said smiling into the microphone.

"I'm so sorry I made a mistake I mixed you girls up with the Notorious Diamonds, I had the final vote and my intentions were to pick you but instead I got you girls confused. I'm so sorry, but you girls are the Winners of the $50,000 and I would be more then happy to have you girls in my video.", Ciara said with Chris Brown jokingly interrupting.

"And I second that!", He said with a goofy look on his face. Frozen in shock—Auriel couldn't say a word, she couldn't believe what she just heard. Sway and Lemon's hands covered their mouths starring at each other in shock with huge smiles on their faces as Lil Bit's jaws dropped. Jumping up in down, surprised shrieking and screaming the girls hugged each other.

"We won we won!", the girls hollered jumping for joy.

"Oh my God! Oh my God!", Lemon said waving her hands uncontrollably. Ciara, Chris Brown, and Free got up form their chairs and walked on stage to congratulate the girls by giving them hugs.

"Oh Chris Chris!", Lemon said frantically and hysterically as her heart hammered in her chest.

"2 weeks ago my baby sister Aniya got shot, she's in the hospital and she loves you sou much. Can you please come with us to go see her.", Lemon said taking heaves of breaths.

"Absolutely!", Chris Brown said.

"Oh thank you thank you Chris Brown. Thank you so much.", Lemon said after she screamed for joy. They did it, the Ladies of Action won.

The next day, surrounding Aniya's hospital bed, Lemon, Sway, Auriel, Lil Bit, Erica, D.J. Lightbulb, and Aniya's mom were happy full of smiles standing and talking with Aniya.

"So what's this big surprise Lemon?", Aniya said. Then there was a knock on Aniya's hospital room's door.

"Somebody is here to see you", The nurse said to Aniya opening the door wider. Taking his hood off, Chris Brown walked to Aniya's hospital bed. "He looks like Chris Brown.", Aniya said to Lemon and her mom.

"I am Chris Brown. How you doing Aniya?", Chris Brown said. Inhaling deeply bucking eyes wide open, Aniya screamed.

"CHRIS BROWN!", Aniya hollered.

"My baby daddy! Take a picture Lemon!", Aniya hollered hugging Chris Brown.

"CHRIS BROWN! CHRIS BROWN!", Aniya repeated. She was so excited and happy that they nurses had to calm her down. Before Lemon could snap a photo Aniya stopped her. "Wait Lemon let me fix my hair for my man!", Aniya said fluffling up her long pretty hair.

Aniya and everyone else took pictures with Chris Brown. He stayed there at the hospital with Aniya for an hour, before he left.

A week later, the girls got their $50,000 check. They were scheduled to fly out to L.A. in 2 weeks to dance in Ciara and Chris Brown's video.

About the Author

Romello Hollingsworth delivers his exciting Hip
Hop Fiction titled: Trying to Live

Printed in the United States
By Bookmasters